THE WRONG MAN

THE WRONG MAN

BRANDON HALL SERIES BOOK 1

MIKE RYAN

WWW.MIKERYANBOOKS.COM

1

He couldn't shake the feeling that he was being followed. Or at the very least being watched. Before getting on the train, he took one last look behind him. Without seeing anything, he just shook it off. Maybe it was the late-night movie he watched the previous night that was doing it to him. It was a thriller in which everyone was out to get the hero, who narrowly escaped at every turn.

Brandon Hall was a twenty-eight-year-old single guy, fresh out of the military, wanting to start his own business. With not having any family to reconnect with, or a wife or girlfriend to come home to, he figured now was the right time to start that business. He had nothing to hold him back. He'd just attended a business conference in San Diego to get some marketing ideas and make some contacts. Since it was only a little over two hours back to Anaheim by train, and since he'd never taken one before, he thought he'd try taking the scenic route back home. Little did he know he was about to embark on a trip he'd never forget.

Once Hall got on the train and found his seat by the window, he put his headphones on and listened to some music as he tried to enjoy the ride. It was a quiet ride for most of the way with the seats next to him and behind him not being taken. Seemed like the train was about three-quarters full. Hall's nice, quiet ride was interrupted with about thirty minutes to go until the train reached the Anaheim station. The empty seat next to him had now been taken, with Hall giving a quick glance at the burly built man with the shaved head and goatee sitting down beside him. Hall then turned his head back toward the window, not giving the man another thought. A few minutes later, Hall felt a tap on his arm. He looked over at the man, who seemed to be giving him a nod like he wanted to talk. Hall took his headphones off and let them drape around the back of his neck as he listened to what the man wanted.

"You need something, man?" Hall pleasantly asked, a smile on his face.

The man didn't reciprocate the friendly tone and looked genuinely upset judging by the scowl on his face that didn't seem to waver. "Where's the stuff?"

"What stuff?"

"You know. Let's not play games, all right? It's a

short ride, let's not make it any longer than we have to."

"I don't know what you're talking about."

"I was told you were cool and could be trusted," the man said, looking even angrier than he did before. "Is that not so?"

Hall sort of shrugged, not really knowing how to answer. He was beginning to think the man had some sort of mental problem. He was certain he'd never seen or interacted with him before. "What do you want?"

"I don't want any problems with you, OK? Just give me the stuff and we can both be on our way."

"What stuff?"

The man looked straight ahead and sighed, deeply annoyed with the games they were playing. Since they were on a train, he was trying to keep his temper under control. He didn't want to lose it in front of a lot of witnesses. Not with what was at stake. He turned his head back toward Hall and tried one more time.

"I'm trying to be patient but I have my limits," the man said. "Just give me the stuff now and we can go our separate ways."

"What stuff? I don't know what you want."

The man let out another sigh, quickly losing the battle with his temper. "I'm about done with this."

"I think you're mistaken about whoever you think I am, man. I'm not whoever it is you're looking for."

"Your name's Hall, isn't it?"

"Yeah."

"Then you're the guy I'm looking for. Palumbo said you were cool but I think he must've lost his mind with you."

"Who's Palumbo?" Hall asked.

"All right, that's it, I'm done."

The man had enough and wasn't about to play any more of the games. He reached into his jacket and pulled out a gun, jamming it into Hall's side. Hall looked on in horror, not sure what was happening. He was frozen, not wanting to make a wrong move with what he assumed was a mentally deranged man. The man saw Hall's black duffel bag and assumed his merchandise was in there. He took a quick look around to make sure they weren't making enough noise to alert any of the other riders. With all the other riders going on about their business, the man then started with his own business.

"Here's what we're gonna do," the man said. "You're gonna grab your bag, then we're gonna walk back into the next car and conduct our business in one of the rooms."

"I don't have any business to conduct with you."

"Well, you're wrong there."

"And I'm not going anywhere with you," Hall said, his voice starting to twitch, highly alarmed with what he thought the man might have planned for him.

"Wrong again. We're both gonna get up, then slowly and calmly walk back to the next car."

"I'm not moving."

The man pushed his gun even further into Hall's side. Hall squirmed a little due to the action, wincing in pain at the discomfort he was experiencing.

"Now you got two choices. You can do what I say and move, or I can pump you full of lead right here."

"You wouldn't do that in the middle of a train."

The man smiled, then let out a small laugh. "Don't try me, kid. You got almost a million dollars of my merchandise in that bag of yours. For that amount of money, I'll deal with the fallout."

"A million dollars?" Hall said, now knowing for sure that there had been a mistake made. "You've got the wrong guy, man."

"I'm not doing this again. Grab your bag and let's go. Or I'll just kill you on the spot."

Hall nodded, ready to finally comply with the man's wishes. He figured it was better to go along with the plot, at least temporarily, then to anger the man any more and risk the consequences. Before the gun-wielding man got up, he had a few last-minute instructions for his guest.

"Just in case you get any ideas, once you get up, look at the seats behind us."

"Why?" Hall asked.

"Because you'll see two more men, both of whom work for me. And just in case you're wondering, they're also carrying guns." Hall just looked at him, knowing what he was implying. "Any sounds, any movements, trying to get away, yelling for help, anything at all...

and they're gonna blow your head off. Right here, right now, no exceptions. They're just gonna come up shooting. Understand?"

Hall nodded that he did, though that didn't seem to be enough for the tough-looking man.

"I wanna hear you say it."

"I understand," Hall replied.

"You better. There's a small kid two rows back to the left of us. I'd hate to ruin his day by getting your blood all over him. Might be traumatic for him."

"I'll do as you ask."

The man smiled, feeling confident, and convinced that Hall was going to behave and do as he asked. "I'm gonna put this gun away, but that doesn't mean you're off the hook yet. Remember, there's two guys behind us."

"I understand."

"Good. Be a good little boy and do what we tell you and you might just live to see tomorrow."

With his gun tucked away, the man stood up, motioning for Hall to do the same. Hall got up and was about to follow, leaving his bag behind. Before he left the area of the seats though, the man motioned for Hall to grab his bag. Hall did, then followed the man into the aisle between the rows of seats. With the black bag in his hand, Hall looked at the seats behind his, observing two more rough-looking men sitting in them. Both of the men stared at him with an evil-looking grin on their face, almost daring him to do something stupid that would give them a reason to use their guns.

A lump went down Hall's throat, wondering what was going on. Why and how was this happening to him? Part of him wanted to back away, run, just about anything to get away from the men, willing to take his chances. But if he believed the man at his word, and they were willing to open fire in the middle of the train, he didn't want to put any other innocent people at risk. Part of the reason he left the military was that he didn't want to engage in violence anymore. After several tours of duty in the Middle East, Hall just wasn't interested in doing that type of stuff now. But just like one of his buddies in the army used to tell him, sometimes the trouble just seems to find you.

Hall continued moving, following the burly man in front of him. As they passed the seats, the two other men also left their seats and started walking behind Hall. As they passed through the passenger cars, Hall still had ideas of fleeing, or turning around and doing some ninja type moves on the men, just like in an action movie. But, still with the other innocent passengers in mind, thought against it. He would just continue doing what the men said until the time was right to do otherwise. He just had to hope that there would be such a time.

As the men passed seats of people, nobody paid much attention to them. Most people were engrossed in conversation, books, music, or their phones, and nobody gave even a second glance to the four men parading through the car. One of the men in back of Hall had a gun jammed into his back to make sure he kept moving. The man had a towel or cloth over top of the weapon to keep it concealed from the public eye.

Once they exited the passenger cars and got to the rooms, the burly man went about halfway down, then unlocked a door to his left. After Hall was led into the room, they placed him near the far wall, his back to the small window. It was a cramped space and couldn't fit much more than the four men already standing in it. With the black bag still in his hand, Hall anxiously awaited for the next set of instructions.

"Open the bag," the burly man said.

One of his cohorts reached down and unzipped it. He opened it and rummaged through it, removing a bunch of clothes and scattering them on the floor. After a minute, the man got back up, frustrated that there was nothing there.

"It's empty," said the man with the glasses.

The burly man was getting angry again. "OK. Where is it? What'd you do with the merchandise?"

Hall didn't know what else to say except what he already had. "I keep telling you I don't know what you're talking about."

The burly man sighed and swiftly removed the gun from his jacket. The other two men did the same. All three men pointed their weapons straight at Hall's chest. Hall put his hands up, fearful of what was about to happen. He worried that he was about to be killed over something he didn't even understand. He survived three tours of duty, seeing action in all of them, and he escaped unscathed. But here he was traveling on a train and he was about to be gunned down over what he assumed was a mistake. Some people say you see your life flash before your eyes when you know you're about to die. But Hall didn't feel or see that at all. His body was growing numb, knowing he still had a lot of living left to do. And it was about to be snatched away from him.

2

As the men continued their conversation, the men with guns were losing their patience. They weren't about to continue this charade much longer.

"I'm gonna give you one last chance," the burly man said.

Hall knew he had to think fast if he was going to make it out of this. "If you kill me now, you're not gonna know where the stuff is."

The burly man smiled. "So you do know. Trying to string us along this whole time with this innocent man crap and the whole time you knew."

"I... uh..."

"Spill it!"

Hall took a deep breath, finally realizing what he had to do. He had to resort to violence again. The thing he'd been trying to move away from. But there was no other way in this instance. It was his only choice.

Though Hall wasn't an especially big man, standing just a shade under six feet and a hundred and ninety pounds, he was in good shape. He wasn't overly muscular, but was strong enough to do most things and athletic enough to do the rest. Considering he was of average appearance, the armed men didn't really consider him much of a threat. Especially with three guns pointing at him. They didn't feel they had much to be alarmed over. That was about to change, though.

Hall began to put his arms down, but was quickly stopped by one of the men, who motioned for him to keep them in the air. He stood there in a somewhat awkward stance, trying to think of how he could use his military training in this situation. He knew he could fight. But considering they had guns, and one of the men could shoot him before he got to all three, he had to think of how he could bring them closer.

"I'm getting tired of standing here, kid," the burly man said. "Let's get this over with so we can all go on with our day."

"If I can put my hands down, I can show you something," Hall replied.

The men looked at each other, not sure what Hall had in mind. But with their eagerness to move on, were willing to let him. They nodded that it was OK for him to lower his arms, which he did.

"It's in the bag," Hall said, starting to reach down for it.

He was quickly stopped, however, with the leader

of the group not sure what he was up to. Part of him thought Hall might have had some kind of trick up his sleeve.

"What are you doing?" the man asked.

Hall stopped his motion and stood up straight again. "Going in the bag."

"For what? It was already checked. There was nothing in there."

Thinking fast, Hall had to play it off, even though he wasn't sure what they were after. "It's not here. You think I'd be dumb enough to carry the stuff with me?"

The burly man wasn't sure what he was talking about. "What do you mean? What else would you do with it?"

"There's a secret compartment on the inside of the bag."

"So? It wouldn't be big enough to hold all the stuff."

Hall shook his head. "No. There's a key inside."

"A key to what?"

"Your merchandise."

"Which is where?"

"In another briefcase."

The burly man didn't look pleased at this mess of games. He was a straightforward kind of guy and didn't appreciate being led around in circles. "In another briefcase where?"

"Let me get the key first and I'll tell you."

Hall started to lean down again, but once again, was stopped before he got to the bag. The men just didn't feel right about him. They thought he was trying to pull a fast one.

"Hold up," the leader said.

"What?" Hall replied.

The burly man looked to one of his partners and nodded, motioning with his gun for him to check the bag instead. The man with the glasses did as was asked and went back to the bag again, kneeling down and putting his hand in it to look for the secret compartment. Hall took a step back and waited for his moment. After a minute of searching, the man still came up empty. He couldn't find a zipper, a pouch, velcro, nothing that would indicate there was another compartment inside the bag. The man looked back at his partners in frustration and slapped his knee before throwing one of his hands up, while the other one was still inside the bag.

"There's nothing here."

The burly man gritted his teeth to try to soothe his anger. "It better be there. What are you trying to push on us?"

Hall feigned a look of surprise at the results. "Hey, it's there, trust me. Can I show him where it's at? Do you mind?"

"Fine. Just do it and get it over with."

"OK."

Hall looked at the man with the glasses, then pointed to the left side of the bag. "It's right there. Just move your hand a little to the right."

The man with the glasses moved his hand as he was told, but still wasn't finding anything but air. Hall knew this was it. This was the moment he needed. He couldn't afford to wait any longer. He wished he had a secret gun stashed in his bag somewhere, but considering he never felt like he would need one again, it would have seemed pointless. But now that he was here, in this ridiculous predicament, he wished he would have taken the extra precaution.

Before doing anything, Hall looked at the two men who still had guns in their hands. Their arms were a little more relaxed, their guns pointed more toward the floor, not appearing to give him as much attention now since they were more concerned about what was in that bag. Hall knew the time was now. The man with the glasses had his head down near the bag as he searched, giving Hall a perfect target.

Hall took one more glance at the two men by the door to make sure they were still in a relaxed position before moving. He slowly moved his right leg back then quickly brought it forward like he was a field goal kicker, delivering a powerful blow to the nose of the glass wearing man. Hall didn't wait to see the result of his blow before lunging toward the others. The other two men reacted slowly as Hall reached them, with him knocking the gun out of the burly man's hand. He then quickly gave a powerful forearm blow to the second man, Hall's elbow catching the man squarely in the jaw, stunning him. As the man stumbled backwards against the wall, Hall turned back around to attack the leader of the group. Instead, he got a punch in the nose that momentarily dazed him.

Hall quickly shook off the blow, then went on his own attack. He delivered a combination of blows, mixing his left and right hands like he was a world-class boxer. With the burly man staggered, Hall turned back around to deliver some more punishment on the other man, who'd regained his senses. Hall blocked a couple of his attempted punches, then dealt a few mixed martial art type of kicks to the man's face and body. As the man hunched over in pain from the beating, Hall grabbed hold of the man's arm and lifted it straight into the air to his side. He then jumped up on the man's side, straddling his legs around the man's chest as he kept a firm grip on the man's arm. In one swift motion, Hall used all of his body weight to drop to the floor, bringing the other man violently down with him as they crashed onto the floor. As they did, the man's arm hyper-extended before Hall also twisted it in a manner which then broke it. It was a move that Hall learned in the army. Though he knew it would work, it wasn't something he ever thought he would actually put into practice. It was something he'd practiced before, but always stopped before going through with the final act.

With the man out of the way, Hall took a quick look at the first man that he kicked, who was still down and holding his nose. By the amount of blood that was now staining the floor, Hall assumed that he had broken it. He wasn't much of a threat at that point, but Hall figured he'd still have to deal with him again before exiting the room. The man with the broken arm was screaming in pain and rolling around in agony, kicking his legs against the floor.

Hall then looked at the burly man, who was just getting up off the floor himself. He'd gotten to his knees, then tried to throw a few more punches at Hall, all of which failed. Hall was really fired up, and the fracas was taking him back to his military days. Now in the heat of battle, there was a crazed look in his eyes that indicated he wasn't going to be defeated.

After sidestepping some of the man's attempted blows, Hall countered with a few shots of his own. With the burly man shaken up, his body was contorted sideways to Hall's position. Hall then took the opportunity to take the man's back, putting his arm underneath the man's throat and forcing him to the ground. Hall put his legs around the man's waist as he continued putting the maneuver on, better known as a rear naked choke in MMA circles. With Hall's arm tucked under his chin, the burly man desperately flailed away at it, frenetically trying to remove it off of his neck before he went under. Only a few short seconds later, the burly man's arms went limp as he drifted off into unconsciousness.

Hall quickly let go of his hold after a few seconds, not wanting to kill the guy. If he'd have kept the hold on for another minute or two, that would have been the end result. But he didn't want to do that. Not unless it was absolutely necessary and there was no other way. At this point, he realized he was a better and tougher fighter than these three. There was no need to kill them. All he wanted to do was stun them long enough to get away.

As Hall got back to his feet, the burly man started to regain consciousness. Hall took another look at the man with the glasses, who was also getting to his feet. Before he was able to stand up all the way, Hall unleashed another superkick, a thrust kick drilling the man directly in the face. It was a move that would make any professional wrestler proud, though there was no letting up with this one. The force of the blow immediately made the man fall onto his back, crushing his broken nose even more.

With two men down and screaming in pain, Hall knew his work was just about done. The burly man was getting to his knees, and Hall sought to finally finish the fight. Hall noticed one of the guns still lying on the ground and picked it up. He calmly walked over to the man and clubbed him hard over the back of his head, blood immediately pouring out from the newly opened gash. The burly man instantly dropped face first onto the ground, holding the back of his head as it throbbed in pain.

Hall dropped the gun as he looked at the three men who were down, none of whom seemed to be in any more of a position to do any damage to him. For good measure though, he delivered another blow to the head of the man whose arm he broke, just to make sure he continued staying down. The other two still didn't seem like much of a problem anymore, so there was no need to bother with them again.

Hall walked over to the door and was about to leave, but took one last look at his fallen opponents. He didn't think it was a good idea to leave them, guns still in hand, though it was questionable how good of a condition they still were in to use them. So Hall walked back over to the gun he'd already dropped and picked it up. He then looked around and saw the other gun on the floor and did the same. Knowing the third man was armed, he walked over to him and frisked him, not getting much opposition. Hall removed the gun and put it inside the belt of his pants.

He looked toward the door again, but couldn't muster the energy to leave just yet. He stood up and continued looking at his victims. They obviously believed he was someone else, but that didn't mean that their business would be through after this. Hall knew it was a distinct possibility that they'd keep coming after him. Even if they realized he was the wrong man, they might try to avenge the beating he just threw down on them. In any case, he knew this might not be the last time he saw them. Either them or people that worked with them.

Whatever the reason, Hall knew he couldn't remain

in the dark. He had to know who or what he was dealing with. He didn't want to ever be surprised again with a situation like this. He then reached down into the man's pocket and removed his wallet. He then walked over to the other two men and did the same. He also removed the key from the burly man's pocket. With all of their wallets and guns in hand, Hall then went to the door. He gave the men one last look, then finally exited the room.

He half-expected to see a group of onlookers waiting there, wondering what all the commotion was about. But nobody was there. Either nobody was in the compartments next to them that could hear what was going on or they were empty for the time being. Regardless, the coast was clear. With the door locked to prevent anyone else from going in, Hall went to the nearest bathroom to clean himself up. Though he didn't sustain too many blows, he knew he must've looked like a sight. He could feel himself sweating and his face was probably red from the exertion. At least with his hair high and tight he didn't have to worry about it being messed up.

Hall's only goal at that point was staying as far away from his attackers as possible until the train stopped. He could have gone to an employee to let them know what happened but he honestly just wanted to distance himself from everything at the moment. He didn't want to press charges, didn't want to deal with the authorities, he didn't want any of that.

He simply wanted to go away and be done with it all. Plus, there was no telling if the three he just roughed up was all there was. For all he knew, there might have been a couple more wandering around the train, just waiting for him. He just wanted to get out of the public view and hide away somewhere until the train stopped and quietly slip away.

As Hall took an unoccupied seat a few cars away, he was breathing a little heavily, still amped up from his skirmish. He tried to catch his breath and slowly was able to control his breathing, calming down slightly. With his mind a little more calm and able to think more clearly, he realized he forgot his bag.

"Crap," he said, wiping his forehead, then the top of his hair.

As he thought of what was in the bag, he realized he had some of his business papers in there. Luckily it was nothing that he couldn't do without or get another copy of. At least he had his wallet and keys with him, so he could at least get in his car and return home. As he continued thinking about the contents of the bag, he remembered that some of his papers included his name and address on them. He ran his hand over his face again, hoping the men wouldn't rifle through his bag once they regained their wits. He sat there for a few more minutes, beating himself up over leaving his bag behind with important information in it. After another minute went by, he knew he had to move on. It was over and done with and there was nothing he could do about it now, other than going back for it. And that just wasn't an option now. He couldn't be sure the bag was still there, or that the men weren't waiting for him, or that he wouldn't run into them or someone else along the way. He had to leave it behind and hope for the best.

Each second that passed by felt like an eternity. Hall looked at the time and saw that they didn't have too much longer before getting to Anaheim. His face started sweating profusely as his nerves started getting the better of him, wondering if there was anything else in store for him before the train stopped. He started wracking his brain, trying to think of a better place to go in case they started searching the train for him. He didn't want to just be sitting there in plain sight. But being as this was his first train ride, he didn't know where else to go, what else might be available.

Hall stood up, not knowing where he was going, but figuring anything was better than just sitting still. It turned out to be a moot point. Almost immediately after standing up, he noticed the burly man looking at him from the end of the car. He and the man with the glasses were just standing there, not yet making a move toward him.

After a stare down of a few seconds between the two parties, the two men took a few steps forward, apparently ready to continue their discussion. Knowing he had no other recourse, except retreating, Hall put his hand inside his jacket and slowly removed one of the guns, just enough for the butt end to show, without alerting any of the other passengers by showing the entire weapon. He just wanted the two men to be aware he had it and let them know he was ready to use it. It worked. After seeing the presence of the gun, the burly man and his companion stopped in their tracks as they contemplated their next move.

With the men stopped for the time being, Hall tucked the gun further away and started walking to the next car, all the while keeping his eyes on the men behind him. The two men didn't make a single move toward following him for the time being. As Hall reached the next car, he took another look behind him, only to see the two men were no longer in sight. He took a deep sigh, thankful he escaped for the moment. But he knew it was only temporary. They'd be back. And now that they realized he was armed, and probably willing to use it, they'd be a little more tactical in approaching him again. But for now, he escaped. And that's all he had going for him at the moment. Living one minute at a time.

3

Once Hall retreated into the next car, he found an empty seat near the front and sat down, still keeping his eyes open. It felt like his head was on a swivel he was looking around so much. His shirt was drenched with perspiration, matching what was falling down his face. He looked down at the time again, hoping he could somehow fast forward the amount that was remaining on the trip.

Hall instinctively looked back to the rear of the car, and to his horror, observed the same two men standing near the door. They stood there for a minute, then calmly took a seat nearby, keeping Hall plainly in their view. Hall wasn't sure what they were planning, but at least they didn't appear to be escalating the situation at the moment.

Hall continued sitting there, looking uncomfortable the entire time. For the most part, he kept his eyes glued to the two men sitting in the back. But he had to keep checking his surroundings, just in case the men had more friends around. And Hall was still a little concerned that the third man was nowhere to be found. He wondered if the man was still in too much pain from his broken arm to proceed with their mission, or whether he was figuring out how and where to ambush him in another spot.

Several more minutes went by without anyone making a move. Everyone stayed in their respective spots, not even a hint of getting up. The burly man and his friend seemed content with how things were playing out. Hall wasn't sure what he was more afraid of, the men making a move now, or knowing they would later. Either way, he knew he wasn't done with them yet.

Nothing happened over the final twenty minutes before the train finally stopped. Once it pulled into the Anaheim station, Hall quickly hopped up out of his seat to exit the train before anyone else. Without having his bag anymore, there was no need for him to wait. He just wanted to put some distance between him and his pursuers.

As more and more passengers got off the train, Hall started putting some more separation between them. He was walking quickly, not wanting to run in case there were others watching. He wasn't sure whether it made any sense to do that, but he thought he'd stand out more if he was running. At least if he walked, he could blend in with other people.

After a few minutes, as more people got off the train, Hall couldn't see the two men anymore. He kept looking back for them, but they disappeared among the throng of people. In reality, the two men had stayed so far back that they weren't even in pursuit of him anymore. They were still walking in Hall's direction, but they didn't have any extra pace in their step. It was almost like they were taking a long, leisurely stroll without any purpose.

"We keep walking like this, we're gonna lose him," the man with the glasses said.

"Don't worry about it," the burly man replied.

"What do you mean, don't worry about it? After everything that happened in there, everything we went through, you're just gonna let him walk out of here with a million bucks of our merchandise?"

"Don't worry about it. He's not getting away with anything."

The bespectacled man was starting to lose it, pointing his finger in Hall's direction. "What do you call that? He's pulling away from us."

"Relax," the sturdy man replied, a smile on his face as if he had no worries. "I told Mac to get some help here pronto. What'd you think he was doing all that time? Putting his arm between his legs and praying?"

"You got more of the boys here?"

"They're watching over the parking lot. They've got

their eyes on Hall. Wherever he goes, we'll be there right behind him."

"You think he pulled a fast one? Maybe he dumped the stuff somewhere before he boarded the train? Then while we were watching him, someone else took the stuff somewhere else?"

"Yeah, could be. Don't matter now. Because now he's a dead man," the well-built man said. "After we get our stuff of course."

When Hall finally got to his car, he hurriedly unlocked the door. Before getting in, he did a three-sixty and looked in every direction, just to make sure no unfriendly people were coming in his direction. With the coast clear, he quickly started the car and pulled away. Little did he know there was another car following him. The new men at the scene had gotten to the station right about the same time as the train arrived. With the description that they were given, they picked up Hall almost immediately after getting off the train and followed him to his car.

Even after exiting the train station parking lot, Hall kept looking in the rear-view mirror, really expecting to see someone following him. He didn't though. He had this wild and crazy notion that he'd wind up getting in some high speed pursuit, just like you would see in an action movie. Even though Hall didn't see anyone behind him, he just wasn't skilled enough to pick them up. The people that were after him had experience with this type of thing. He wasn't the first person they tailed in a manner like this. They knew how to stay back, switch lanes, make themselves inconspicuous. They were more skilled than Hall was at this type of work.

As the men tailed Hall, they kept their boss up to date on their progress, letting him know which direction they were going. The three men from the train station had gotten in a car as well and were also on their way. The car following Hall did get close enough to read his license plate. They relayed that info back to the leader of the group. The brawny man immediately got out his phone and called another of his men, passing on the plate number. After a few minutes, the man had what he wanted. He then called one of the men in the car behind Hall.

"Yeah?"

"I got his address," the burly man said. "Break off and get to his place first. Wait there for him."

"What if he don't go there?"

"Well that's the direction he's heading. I want you guys to be there ahead of him. Throw him a little surprise party."

"I hope you're sure, because if he figures his place is being watched, and he bugs out somewhere else, we might not be able to pick him out again."

"Relax. As far as he knows, he's gotten away clean. There's no reason for him to think we know where he lives. Even if he does, he's probably gonna pack up first."

"But what if he packed up already?"

"Well then he wouldn't still be going in the direction of his apartment numb nuts. He would've already split. Now pay attention and do what I tell you and stop arguing."

"I'm not arguing, I'm just throwing out ideas."

"Well stop it," the hefty man replied. "You're not getting paid to think. You get paid to do what I tell ya. Now listen up."

"All right, all right. Sheesh."

"Now he lives in an apartment. I want you guys to get in there and find a good spot to hide. Let him get situated at first. Maybe he'll say or do something to indicate where he put the stuff at."

"He lives in an apartment, man. How many places to hide can there be?"

"Just do what I tell you and stop back-talking. Make sure he doesn't spot you the moment he comes in or anything. Just lay low."

"All right, all right, we'll lay low."

"And stop rolling your eyes and mumbling under your breath 'cause I know you're doing it."

"I swear I wasn't..."

"Yeah, yeah, just stop lollygagging and get your lazy...." Just as the burly man was about to let loose with a few curse words towards his associate, a horn from a nearby truck completely drowned his voice out, making his words inaudible.

"We're on our way! We'll get there first."

The burly man hung up and put his phone in his pocket, mumbling a few choice words himself. "Stupid idiots."

"What's a matter?" the glass wearing man asked.

"Stupid idiots. Always questioning things, always making remarks, always throwing out their own ideas." As he complained about his men, he threw his hands and arms in the air for emphasis, waving them around. "Dumb stupid idiots."

"They're OK sometimes."

"They're buffoons. After this job's over, remind me to get rid of them."

"Get rid of them? What for?"

"Because they're idiots."

"You just need to cool down a little bit. Once this is over and we get the money, you'll change your mind."

"I hope not."

"They're loyal, Rex. Maybe not the smartest group in the barrel, and maybe they complain a little more than they should, but they always show up and do what you want."

"Yeah, after me telling them a couple of times. And after listening to their own ideas."

"Still, they always do it."

"Yeah, yeah, enough talk about them slobs. Let's hurry up and get to Hall's apartment."

"What're you gonna do when we get there?"

"Same as we did before," the well-built man answered. "We never finished our conversation from the train. And I think our friend needs a little heavier reminder."

"What if he still don't tell us nothin'?"

"We'll make him talk. We'll have five guys there instead of three. He won't get the jump on us this time. This time we'll be ready for him."

"Four guys really," the glass wearing man said. "Benny really ain't gonna be any good with his arm broke."

The burly man turned his head around and looked at the back seat, where Benny was still holding his arm, in obvious pain.

"As soon as this is over, Ben, we'll get you to a hospital or something. You're gonna have to hold on."

"I'm good, Rex. I can wait."

"Good man."

They were about twenty minutes away from Hall's apartment at that point. They figured they were about five to eight minutes behind their target. It didn't leave a lot of time for their friends to get to Hall's apartment first. But Rex was confident they would do it. As much as he complained about his associates, they really never did let him down. At least not anything major.

About five minutes later, Rex got a message from his associates that they'd just arrived at Hall's apartment. The burly man let them know they didn't have much time to get inside. According to his calculations, Hall was probably only five or six minutes behind them. And they were about five minutes behind Hall.

The two men were in the hallway, just outside of Hall's door. They had to wait a minute for a couple of people to pass before getting to work on the lock. Once the coast was clear, they went to work. They had the door open in less than a minute, obviously not their first time doing such an act. Once inside the apartment, they locked the door again and started looking around. They were careful to not touch or move anything that would alert Hall that someone else was there.

Knowing they didn't have much time to waste, the two men quickly found a couple of hiding spots. They each took up a position in a different room to wait. Almost exactly five minutes later, Hall came walking through the door. After closing and locking the door, he stood behind it for a minute and looked through the peephole, just to see if anyone was closing in. With nobody there, Hall then went over to the window and looked down from his third-floor window at the partial view of the lot. He didn't see anything out of the ordinary. He'd only been at the apartment for around a month or so, but it always seemed to be a pretty quiet complex. There never seemed to be any trouble or menacing looking people hanging around.

After looking out the window a few minutes, Hall started to think maybe he'd actually gotten away from the group chasing him. He stood there in his living room, just thinking about everything that happened in the past couple of hours. As it sunk in, he started feeling uneasy being there. If they knew his name, they would probably find out his address, if they hadn't already. He wondered how he got into this mess. Maybe there was a second Brandon Hall that the men were looking for. That would have been a major coincidence and an unbelievable stroke of bad luck if there were.

Hall nervously sat on the edge of his couch as he considered his options. Ultimately, he decided the best thing to do was just go to the police and tell them what happened. Maybe they could make heads or tails out of what was going on. He certainly didn't have any answers. And if the men were after him and continued to chase him, he didn't know how long he could hold out or escape from them. He went to the kitchen and got himself a cold beer and took a few sips as he stood in the kitchen, pondering his future. As it stood at the moment, it didn't seem like he had much of one.

4

Once Hall finished his beer, he was going to go down to the police station and tell them his story. Before that though, he took a trip to the bathroom. As he walked down the short hallway of his one bedroom, one bath apartment, he glanced at his bedroom door. He thought it was strange. The door to his bedroom was closed and he almost always left it open. Every now and then he'd close it if he wasn't really thinking or he had something else on his mind, but for the most part, he liked having the door open. He thought back to a few days ago when he first left for his trip and he was almost positive that he left it open.

Hall gently pushed the door open and stood there, peering into the room cautiously, thinking that maybe someone was in there. There weren't many places to hide. Under the bed and inside the walk-in closet were about it. Everything seemed to be the way he left it though, so he thought maybe it was just his mind playing tricks on him. He then went into the bathroom and immediately was startled by the shower curtain. It was also closed. Now he knew someone was there. He always left the shower curtain open when it wasn't in use. Ever since he saw a scary movie as a little boy, he always had a fear of someone hiding behind a shower curtain on him. Anytime he entered a bathroom that had a shower curtain, he always had a habit of peeking inside, just to alleviate his fears. He would never leave it closed, not even if his mind was on other things.

He flipped the bathroom light on and then turned on the water in the sink. He wanted whoever was there to make them think he was busy and not yet alerted to their presence. Hall inched closer to the shower, careful not to move too fast and give himself away. He put his arm up to the curtain, not yet touching it. He then grabbed the edge of the curtain and quickly yanked it open, revealing the presence of a strange man inside.

The strange man seemed to be the more startled between the two of them. Hall quickly grabbed hold of the man's arm and did a judo flip, tossing the man out of the shower. The man landed on his back, his head glancing off the base of the toilet. Hall put his hands around the man's head to get him back to his feet so he could unleash some more punishment. Hall hit him with some kicks, punches, and a few karate moves. The man was in complete disarray and wasn't even competitive in their fight. Hall continued his assault before finally finishing the contest. He took hold of the man's head and rammed it against the toilet bowl, rendering the man completely useless and out of the fight. Though the stranger wasn't yet unconscious, he was beaten to a pulp, and likely wouldn't get back up for an hour.

Though this fight was finished, Hall knew the battle probably wasn't over. While the man lay on the floor motionless, Hall's thoughts turned back to the bedroom. He thought it likely someone was in there now too. There was no other explanation for the door being closed. Hall slowly emerged from the bathroom. As soon as he turned the corner, he was met with a thundering punch that caught him flush on the forehead. The blow stunned Hall momentarily and made him lose his balance, causing him to stumble backwards, hitting the wall.

Though the punch did some damage, Hall still never lost his feet underneath him. As the man came closer to him to deliver some more bad news, Hall got the jump on him, nailing him with a few shots to the stomach and kidneys. Hall then got in a few kicks, also getting the man in the side, which seemed to be a weak spot for him. After a few minutes of mostly absorbing punishment, the man knew he wasn't going to win a hand-to-hand combat fight with Hall. In an effort to cut the melee short, the man reached behind him and removed his gun. He brought it around to the front and briefly pointed it at his target, but Hall quickly knocked it away before he was able to get a good aim. The gun flew out of his hand and knocked against the wall before settling on the floor.

The man tried to reach down for it, but Hall had other ideas in mind. He continued railing against him, alternating between boxing and martial arts against the mismatched fellow. After a few more minutes, Hall completely had the upper hand and grabbed hold of the man's neck. With all his might, Hall threw the man's head into the drywall, creating a huge indentation as the man's head went through the wall. The man was completely out of the fight by now and Hall tugged on his shirt to bring him back to within range. The man was barely able to stand and wobbled on his feet. Hall gave the man one more shot to the face, instantly knocking him to the floor. The man was stunned and no longer an issue.

With not knowing if there was anybody else there in the apartment, all Hall wanted to do at the moment was escape. Though he had gotten the upper hand, he knew he couldn't do that forever, especially if they eventually outnumbered him. He just had to get away. He didn't know where, but anywhere would be better right now. Hall scurried over to the front door, hoping he wouldn't get stopped by another intruder along the way. Once he got to the door, he stopped and looked back at his apartment. He was trying to think if there was anything in there that he needed. He didn't know when, or if, he'd be back, so if there was anything indispensable to him, he needed to grab it now. But he didn't have long to think about it. He knew those two goons wouldn't stay down forever. After some brief thought, he couldn't think of anything he needed.

Hall opened the door and flew down the hallway. He rushed over to the elevator, waiting for it to open. After a brief wait, the door finally opened. Hall's eyes widened as he was shocked to see the same glass wearing man as was on the train. As the two stared at each other, Hall rushed into the elevator, spearing the man in the gut as they settled against the wall. They wrestled around on their feet, one of them eventually hitting one of the elevator buttons by accident. They continued wrestling, as well as punching, as the elevator made its way back down to the ground floor.

By the time the elevator stopped, Hall had come out on top once again. The man with the glasses was lying down face first, courtesy of a Hall back kick to the face. When the doors finally opened, Hall rushed out and ran down the hallway until he came to the front doors. Before he opened the inner glass doors, he looked beyond them and saw the burly man coming in, and the broken-armed man right behind him. They saw him too.

Hall quickly back stepped and ran back down the hallway in the other direction, toward the stairs. The other men rapidly threw the door open and rushed inside, in hot pursuit of their man. As the burly man came inside, he looked to his left and saw the opened elevator, with his man still lying on the floor.

"Benny, go check on Rick," the leader ordered.

The broken-armed man did as he was directed and went over to the elevator to check on his friend's condition. Still breathing, he helped the man to his feet. They then left the elevator and walked over to the stairs, where their boss was waiting for him. He was just standing at the base of the steps, looking up.

"Well, there's only three floors, so there's not many places for him to go," Rex said.

"You think the other guys found him yet?" Benny asked.

"Unfortunately, I'd say that's a good probability."

"So what do you wanna do?"

"We need to cut him off. I'll go up the steps and check each level. Benny, you stay down here by the door and make sure he don't go out. Ricky, you take the elevator and check each level too."

Ricky, the glass wearing man, didn't really like the idea. Hall had already proven he was individually tougher than all of them. He'd already taken each of them out. Breaking up to look for him was a mistake in his mind. They needed to stay together, he thought. There was more strength in having numbers on their side.

"What is it?" Rex asked, reading his partner's face, which quite obviously gave away his displeasure.

"It's just..."

"Just what?"

"We're all breaking up to find this guy."

"So?"

"So he's already beaten us all to kingdom come," Ricky said. "He broke Benny's arm, I think he broke my nose, he put you unconscious, who knows what he did to the boys upstairs, face it, Rex, he's tougher than we are."

"So what do you wanna do? Give up and go home?"

"No, but breaking up and going after him individually ain't gonna work. He'll take us all apart one at a time if that happens."

"It's the only thing we can do right now," Rex replied. "There's too many ways he can get out of here if we don't block all the exits for him."

Ricky rolled his eyes, still not liking the plan, but knowing he wasn't going to change his boss' mind. He rarely could when it was set like this.

"Besides, he's not that tough," Rex said. "He got us by surprise back on the train. He couldn't do that again if we were all paying attention more."

Ricky turned his head and rolled his eyes again, thinking his boss was out of his mind. Yeah, Hall might have surprised them slightly, but at this point, if any of them didn't think Hall was tougher than them, they weren't paying attention. But nonetheless, he did as was expected of him and went back to the elevator as Benny stationed himself by the front door, still holding his arm. But each of the men, other than Rex, honestly hoped they didn't run into Hall again. They didn't think they could survive another encounter with him. Not without Hall doing even more damage to them.

Hall immediately went back up to the third floor. He didn't know where else to go. He assumed they would check the second floor first before proceeding to the top floor. But there was nowhere for him to go on the second floor. He didn't know anyone, and there was no place for him to hide. Not that things were much better on the third floor. It was pretty much the same thing. He couldn't go back to his apartment with the thugs still there, and who knew how much longer they would be incapacitated. Even if he got inside his apartment and called the police, it could be a long wait until they arrived. And maybe they'd get there too late.

Hall stood just inside the hallway after exiting the stairwell, taking a few deep breaths as he contemplated his next move. He wasn't sure what to do. He knew there wasn't much time left until the men found him. Part of him thought the best thing to do was just stand there and wait for them. He'd bested them in hand-to-hand combat so far. He had to hope he could keep it up.

As he stood there, waiting for the men to arrive, Hall heard a nearby door open up. He snapped his head back in that direction, fearing that it might have been the two men coming out of his apartment. It wasn't though. It was Charlotte Sabo. She lived two doors down from Hall and on the opposite side. He didn't know her that well, though they'd had a couple of brief conversations in the hall as they were coming or going. Hall actually didn't know a thing about her personally, other than she liked cats and animals.

Charlotte was twenty-six years old and had lived at the apartment for close to two years. She was a hard-working single woman who chose to spend much of her free time by herself. She had friends, including some close ones, but she wasn't very much into the party scene. She was a pretty enough woman, with long blonde hair, and an attractive figure, but she didn't like flaunting herself at clubs or bars in hopes of attracting someone. She much preferred quiet, intimate settings, time alone, just hanging around her apartment watching TV or reading. And she was OK with all of that. She didn't need being with a boyfriend to make her happy. She was quite content with her life as it was. If she ever met someone, that was fine, but she didn't intend to ever go out of her way to meet someone.

As Charlotte was exiting her apartment, she saw Hall standing by the stairs and flashed him a smile before starting to lock her door. She was a pretty girl, Hall thought. And the brief times that they'd talked, Hall always thought she seemed nice enough. She didn't seem self-absorbed or artificial in any way. Just a nice, sweet girl. As she was locking her door, Hall's eyes darted toward the elevator, seeing the light flash on the third floor. Hall then turned his head back to the stairs, hearing what sounded like heavy footsteps approaching. If something was about to go down in the hallway, he didn't want Charlotte to wind up getting mixed up in it and possibly get hurt. Hall rushed over to her door, and just as Charlotte turned around, he pushed her back against the door.

"Hey, what is this?" she asked "What's going on?"

"I'll tell you in a minute, just get inside," Hall replied, frantically looking to both sides as he awaited his visitors.

"Why, what's going on?"

Hall was getting nervous they were about to be interrupted before he could get Charlotte to safety. He was more worried about her than he was himself. He could handle himself, but he knew these guys meant business, and they'd probably have no second thoughts about hurting an innocent person along with him.

"Hurry up and get back inside before trouble gets here."

"Trouble? What are you talking about?" Charlotte asked.

Hall wiped his forehead, then took another peek in both directions. He quickly grabbed the keys out of her hand and put the key in the lock. She protested what he was doing, but he didn't pay any attention to her. He continued what he was doing and opened the door, then grabbed her by the arm and shoved her back inside, with him following her in.

Just as he closed the door, the elevator opened, the glass wearing man stepping out. Then the burly man emerged from the stairwell. They looked at each other and shrugged, not sure what happened. They didn't think they could have missed him. They met in the middle of the hall and discussed where he was.

"I'll check his apartment," Rex said. "You check the roof."

"Right."

As Rex went into Hall's apartment, he immediately noticed his men, who were still down and out. Hall was looking through the peephole of Charlotte's door and saw the glass wearing man go by. Charlotte had taken a few steps back, slightly alarmed by Hall's behavior. A small piece of her worried that he was going to try to do something to her. She tried to shrug those thoughts off though, as he seemed more concerned about whatever was happening on the outside of the door.

Charlotte put aside any thoughts about her being harmed and was brave enough to walk back to the door, standing right next to Hall. She demanded to know what was going on.

"Just what is..."

Her voice was soon muted as Hall immediately put his hand over her mouth to silence her. Though she wasn't talking loudly, he didn't want to take the chance of her voice alerting the men outside. Charlotte initially struggled to get free of him, but Hall grabbed hold of her and pinned her to the wall. Now she really had some improper thoughts going through her mind. Hall took a quick peek down at her and saw the scared look on her face and slowly removed his hand from her mouth. He put his index finger over his lips to let her know it wasn't safe to talk yet. After she nodded her head, Hall looked back through the peephole.

A few minutes later, he saw several of the men convening in the hallway, discussing the situation. There were the two men he beat up in his apartment and the man who wore glasses. After a couple more minutes, the burly man came by with his partner, who still was holding his arm. Now the group was complete. Hall put his ear to the door to try to hear their conversation.

"So where'd he go?" Benny asked.

"Yeah, it's like he disappeared," Ricky replied.

"He didn't disappear," Rex said. "It's obvious he ducked in another apartment somewhere. There are no other ways out. He didn't jump off the roof, and he didn't go back downstairs or jump out a window. He's hiding somewhere. We need to find him."

"How we gonna do that? Start breaking into apartments?"

"Start knocking on doors. Two guys on the first floor in case he heads down there, two guys on the second floor, then I'll take up here."

As the guys split up and went their separate directions, Hall finally unglued himself from the door. He backpedaled as he contemplated what he was going to do. With his eyes solely fixed on the door, Charlotte could see he had other things on his mind. He wasn't the least bit concerned about her. She took the opportunity to turn around and look through the peephole herself, though she didn't see anything out there. She started to think the nice-looking guy was out of his mind.

"You wanna tell me what's going on now?" Charlotte asked.

Hall deeply sighed as he looked around, just wanting to be done with everything. He rubbed his eyes and then wiped the sweat forming on his forehead. Charlotte could tell by the look on his face, and his mannerisms, that the man standing in front of her was deeply concerned about something.

"Are you hiding from the cops?"

Hall shook his head. "No. I'm not wanted for anything. There's some bad people out there looking for me."

"Why? What did you do?"

"I haven't done anything. I think they mistook me for somebody else. They first got me on the train here, then I found people in my apartment when I got home. I don't know what they want."

Charlotte looked at him with a slither of disbelief. Though he certainly seemed sincere, these kinds of things just didn't happen in real life. It was only a movie plot. But still, he really did give off the vibe that he was being hunted by someone.

"In a few minutes there's gonna be a knock on your door," Hall said. "Just tell them you don't know me. I was never here."

"Hey, if you're mixed up in something, I don't really wanna get involved in it."

"I don't blame you. I'm just afraid that if they find me in here, they might think you are mixed up in it. I don't want something to happen to you too. Trust me, as soon as they're gone, I'll be on my way."

Charlotte tried to pry some more details out of him, but Hall was reluctant to tell her anything else. The less she knew the better off she was as far as he was concerned. All she needed to know was just enough for her not to freak out until he was gone. After a few minutes had gone by, they were both startled by a loud knock on the door. Hall went into the kitchen, hiding behind a half-wall as Charlotte went to answer the door. Before answering though, she scurried into the kitchen for a final word with Hall.

"Why do I even need to answer it at all?" she whispered. "Why not just let them knock and think nobody's here?"

"Because if they already heard someone moving around in here, they're gonna think something's up. And if they hang around and then see you leaving later, they're gonna think you were hiding from them because you know me or something. It's better to just answer and get rid of them."

"Oh. OK."

"Can you do that?"

"Yeah, I guess so," Charlotte replied, still not sure whether she wanted to. "Are you sure you're not a criminal or something?"

"If I was, do you really think I'd be here trying to explain it to you?"

"No, I guess not."

Charlotte then left and shuffled to the door. After a few more knocks, she finally opened the door. She only opened it a little, just enough for her head to be visible as the rest of her body was hidden behind it. She saw a large man standing there, trying to look friendly, though it seemed to her that it was something he didn't do very often. He looked as though he was uncomfortable trying to be pleasant.

"Yes? Can I help you?" Charlotte politely asked.

The man took a police badge out of his pocket and flashed it at her. "Yes, ma'am, I'm with the police, have you seen the man that lives across the hall there, just a few doors down?" Rex pointed at Hall's door.

Charlotte poked her head out of the door a little further to see where he was pointing. "Uh, no, no I haven't. Why? What's this about?"

"He's a person of interest in a crime that happened earlier today and we'd like to talk to him about it. So far he's eluded us and we saw him in the building a little while ago."

"Oh. Did he actually do something?"

"Well, I'm afraid I can't really talk too much about

it now, ma'am. It's an official investigation so I can't really say too much."

"Oh, I understand."

"So he hasn't been here or anything?"

"No, he hasn't. I don't really know him that well though. If he needed help, he wouldn't come to me."

"OK. Does he have any other friends in the building or places that he would go?"

"I really wouldn't know," Charlotte answered. "I'm sorry."

"No problem. Thanks for your time."

"Sure."

As soon as Charlotte closed the door, Rex instinctively looked down, observing the handle on the door. He noticed what looked like a small stain on it. He bent down to get a better look at it. He swiped his finger over it, getting a small batch of red liquid on his finger. He rubbed it between his index finger and his thumb as he brought it closer to his eyes. It was blood. Considering they'd all been roughed up by Hall, and several of them were bleeding, it must have been Hall's blood.

Rex took a few steps to the side and just stood there with his back against the wall. He continued looking at the door, trying to figure out all the ways the blood could have gotten on there. He eventually came to two conclusions. Either Hall touched the handle of the door as he was passing by, or, he was inside that apartment. Rex pulled out his phone and started calling all his partners.

"Anybody get anything?"

He received a negative reply from everybody, giving even more credence to his assumption that Hall was inside the woman's apartment. Rex continued staring at the door, though he now stood several feet away, out of range of anyone seeing him through the peephole of Charlotte's door. The more he thought about everything that had happened up to that point, the more convinced he became that the man he was looking for was only a few feet away.

5

After looking through the peephole and seeing that the man was gone, Charlotte immediately went back over to her visitor. She had even more questions now.

"I thought you said they weren't cops?"

"They're not," Hall said, standing back up straight.

"That guy flashed me a badge. He talked like he was a detective or something."

Hall vehemently shook his head. "No, he's not. He can't be."

Charlotte just stared at him, a look in her eye like she didn't quite believe him now. Wanting to prove what he was saying was true, Hall reached into his pocket and pulled out the wallets that he took from the men on the train.

"They're not, look," Hall said, walking over to the kitchen table and setting the wallets on it.

He sat down, and Charlotte did the same, though directly across from him, still not wanting to get that close if she could help it. Hall opened each wallet, read the name, then passed it across the table so she could look at it.

"How'd you get these?" Charlotte asked.

Hall looked almost embarrassed to say. "Well, we had a little altercation in a room and before I left, I took them."

"You took their wallets?"

"I wanted to see who I was dealing with. They seemed to know everything about me already."

"What'd you do, knock them all out first?"

"Well.... anyway, that's not the point," Hall answered. "The point is, look at their wallets. Not a single mention of them being police officers. He probably flashed you a phony badge so you wouldn't get scared to talk to him or call the real cops."

"I don't know."

Hall went over to the window to look down below. He didn't expect to see anything though, as it was a small patch of grass, some benches, and a few walking paths, that then led up to another building. There were a few people sitting on benches, but he recognized them as people that lived there, seeing them several times before.

"Whatever's happening here, I don't know," Charlotte said. "But if what you're saying is true, you need to go to the police and explain it."

"I would love to if I could get there."

"Just pick up the phone and have a patrol car come here and tell them your story."

"Part of me feels like there's nothing they can do. It's just my word."

"You gotta start somewhere. And you can't stay here all day."

"Yeah, I guess you're right," Hall said. "Hope they don't think I stole these wallets or something."

"That's not all you better hope."

"What do you mean?"

"You also better hope they're not really police officers. Because if they are, I'd say you're in a lot of trouble. Probably assault, not to mention stealing their identification."

A lump went down Hall's throat. Though he was pretty certain that they weren't police officers, he still couldn't say that with a hundred percent conviction. What if he made a major mistake, and they really were? What if he got himself mixed up in some kind of undercover operation? Whatever the case was, the one thing he did know, he was in a big mess. After thinking about it for a few minutes, he thought the best thing to do was to just try to figure things out on his own before enlisting anybody else's help.

"Maybe I'll just wait a little bit," Hall said.

Charlotte grinned. "You're not really sure, are you?"

Hall put his hands on top of his head as he put his elbows on the table. "I'm not really sure what's going on anymore. My head's spinning. All I did was go to a conference in San Diego. I hop on the train to come home, then all this stuff happens."

Charlotte stared at him for a minute, seeing that he was obviously upset by everything. Maybe he really was leveling with her, she thought. He seemed genuine in his reaction to everything. He didn't seem like he was trying to pull something over on her. Hall stayed seated for another minute, before figuring it was time to go. He got up and put the wallets back in his pocket.

"Well, I've taken up too much of your time already," Hall said. "Thanks for letting me crash here for a little bit."

"So what are you gonna do? Where are you gonna go?"

Hall shrugged. "I don't know. I need to figure out what exactly's going on and who these people are. I got their wallets, guess I need to go on the internet and plug their names in to find out who they are."

Charlotte couldn't believe what was about to come out of her mouth. "Well, I've got a laptop over there if you want to use it."

Hall put his hand up, appreciating the gesture, but not about to spend any more time there. The longer he was there, the more jeopardy he put her in. He walked to the door, Charlotte right behind him.

"Do you have any other friends or family who can help you?" Charlotte asked.

"No, not really. I just got out of the military not too

long ago. My parents live back east and I was last stationed in San Diego, so I just decided to stay out this way. I don't know too many other people here other than some of my military buddies."

"Can't they help?"

"They're all back in San Diego living on the base."

Hall was ready to leave and had gotten to the door, but was interrupted before he had a chance to open it.

"Umm, do you want me to, uh, like check around, make sure they're gone and all?" Charlotte asked.

Hall smiled. "Thanks, but you've done enough for me already. I don't need or want you to take more chances for me."

"OK. Well, I guess take care of yourself."

"Thanks. You too."

Just as Hall turned back toward the door, it violently came crashing open, thanks to two of Rex's men thrusting themselves into it. Charlotte let out a scream as she scurried into the kitchen, away from the action. With the two men on the ground, Hall took the opportunity to keep them there, delivering a punch to each of the back of their heads. As he was preoccupied, the burly man then came in, taking Hall by surprise.

Rex nailed Hall in the back of the head, causing him to stumble to his knees. Knowing how much trouble he was in, Hall quickly got back up, shrugging off the pain like it was nothing. Rex removed his gun and pointed it at him, but Hall kicked it out of his hand. They then engaged in another scuffle, eventually falling to the floor as they rolled around, knocking a lamp, some magazines, along with a couple of collectibles off a table. As they rolled around, the other two men got back to their feet. They then went over to where the tussle was happening and pulled Hall off their leader.

As Hall was brought back to his feet, the two men grabbed hold of his arms and held them behind his back. Rex took the opportunity to inflict some damage on him, while he was restrained, alternating punches as he struck Hall's rib cage.

"You gonna tell us where the stuff's at?" Rex said as he continued pounding away.

He stopped the beating just long enough for Hall to reply. "Told you, I don't know what you're talking about."

"Wrong answer."

Rex continued his assault, his punches now alternating between Hall's midsection and his face. Charlotte had been watching the entire scene unfold from the kitchen. She was hardly able to watch as Hall was slowly being taken apart. She was now definitely believing Hall's story, since the men beating him didn't appear to be acting like any police officer she'd ever seen or heard of. Charlotte then appeared from the kitchen, drawing a look from Rex.

"You guys aren't cops, are you?" she asked.

Rex looked at one of his men, then nodded in the woman's direction, wanting them to take care of her. As one of the men let go of Hall's arm, he fell down to the floor as the other two continued hitting him. As the third man approached her, Charlotte started backing up, getting a bad vibe from his presence. She let out another high-pitched scream as the man lunged at her. Charlotte successfully evaded him at first, running around the table until she stumbled and fell on the floor. She quickly got back to her feet, though she was now cornered and couldn't escape. With the man moving in, she frantically looked around for anything she could use to fend the man off.

The man practically jumped on top of her, straddling her up against the counter. Though the man was trying to control her arms, Charlotte kept swinging them wildly, slapping the man in the face, head, back, anything and anywhere that would help her get loose. After a minute of fighting, she knew she was losing the battle and needed some extra help. She saw a frying pan on the stove that she used to make her lunch. The man had a good grip on her, but with her continuing to flail away, she was able to slither herself down the counter until she got within range of the pan. She got her fingers on it for a moment before it got away from her as she wriggled around with the strange man. After struggling for another minute to get her hands on it, she finally was able to wrap her fingers around the handle.

The man had his head down to avoid getting slapped in the face again and didn't notice that Charlotte now had control of the pan. With a firm grip on the pan, Charlotte took a full size swing at the back of the man's head, hitting him hard. With the unsuspecting wallop, the man fell to his knees, finally relinquishing control of his victim. He let out a moan as he held his head. He then looked up at Charlotte, just in time to see her taking a two handed swing with the pan, connecting across the left side of his face, instantly cutting him above his eye and bruising his cheek. The man dropped fully to the ground as he was just about out of it.

Charlotte wasn't going to take any chances with him though. Her father had always told her that if she was ever attacked, to defend herself vigorously, that she should never assume that she'd won if she got the man down. He taught her that if she got an attacker down, to make sure he stays there, by whatever means necessary. They'd even playfully practiced a few scenarios, just so her dad could be sure that she knew how to defend herself, which was always a concern of his once she moved out of the house when she was done college. Though she thankfully never had to put it into practice before now, she never forgot the lessons. They always stuck in her mind.

With the man down, Charlotte could see that he wasn't knocked out yet, which was her goal for the moment. If he was still moving, he was still a threat as far as she was concerned. She re-gripped the handle of the pan and swung it vociferously at the man's head, striking him repeatedly on the back of it. She kept repeating the motion, hammering the man until he was no longer moving. Satisfied that he was no longer an issue, Charlotte moved closer to the half-wall that separated the kitchen and main living area.

"What the hell's taking him so long in there?" Rex asked. He then yelled into the kitchen. "What are you doing in there, Johnny? Getting your groove on? Come on, hurry up. You can do that later."

After a few seconds with no response, Rex was tired of the wait and sent in the other man to check on him. He continued whaling away on Hall as the other man left. The second man walked into the kitchen, no worries on his mind as to what he was about to find and run into. As soon as he turned the corner, Charlotte thumped him with the frying pan. She took a two-handed grip and clubbed him square in the face, immediately dropping him to the ground. As the man writhed around in pain, she continued hitting him. Blood squirted out from his nose, which had broken with her first hit. As he screamed in pain and put his arms up to protect his head, Rex looked up and saw what was happening.

"What the hell is this? You telling me both you guys got beat up by a girl?"

He sighed and stopped his assault on Hall to see what was going on. He cautiously approached the kitchen, ready for the woman to try that trick with him. Just as he suspected, as soon as he walked in, she tried to nail him with the pan. He was ready for it though and blocked the blow. A mean scowl enveloped his face as he stared into Charlotte's eyes. Rex then snatched the pan away from her hands and tossed it onto the floor on the other side of the kitchen.

"Think you're a tough girl, huh?" Rex said. His menacing presence caused Charlotte to backtrack. "What are you gonna do now, huh?"

After a few seconds, she finally stopped moving backwards and stood still. "Nothing." Rex smiled, thinking he had the situation under control. Charlotte's eyes moved past the man in front of her and looked over his shoulder, observing Hall moving in behind him. She then pointed behind him. "He might, though."

Rex smiled and chuckled. "That's the oldest trick in the book, lady. I'm not falling for that one. You're gonna have to do better than that."

Hall then tapped him on the back of his shoulder. A concerned look came over Rex's face, hoping it wasn't what he thought it was. He quickly turned around, ready to unleash some more punishment. He tried to throw a right-hand roundhouse punch as he turned, but Hall easily saw it coming and ducked in time.

Hall then kicked his opponent in the sides, stomach, and chest, before unloading with some punches to the man's face. Hall got him in a headlock, then used his momentum to get his adversary to the ground.

After another minute of grappling, Hall let go of the headlock and switched to an armbar. Hall then tucked Rex's arm behind him and pulled him, fully trying to break his arm. His intentions were interrupted though, as Charlotte came running in full blast, frying pan in hand. She swung with all her might, drilling Rex in the head with the cooking instrument, knocking him out cold.

Hall could feel the man's body go limp and knew he was out. He then let go of his hold and stood up. It was actually the best result for Rex, as Hall would have surely broken his arm had Charlotte not knocked him out. If she hadn't, he definitely would have had his arm broken. Now, he was just going to wake up with a nasty headache. But at least all his body parts were in one piece. As Hall stood up and looked at the body in front of them, he complimented Charlotte on her skills.

"You swing a pretty good frying pan."

Charlotte smiled, appreciating the compliment. "Thanks. I played softball in high school."

"I can tell."

They both stood there breathing heavily, trying to come down from the rush of the fracas they were just involved with. Hall went into the kitchen to make sure the other two men wouldn't still be a problem, but they were both knocked out too. They at least had a few minutes now to collect themselves and figure out their next step. Charlotte had her hands on top of her head, scarcely believing what just happened. She looked around and saw three bodies lying around her apartment.

"All right, I know there's at least two more of them," Hall said.

"OK. So what are we gonna do?"

"Well if you want, call the police and tell them what happened."

"What are you gonna do?"

"Gonna find the other two."

"Wait, you can't leave me alone with these guys up here," Charlotte protested.

"They're knocked out."

"What if they don't stay that way by the time the police get here?"

"Go to a neighbor's place and wait," Hall answered.

"And what if they follow me there?"

Hall shrugged, not having any other answers for her. "I dunno. Just go anywhere then."

"I think the best thing right now is to just go where you're going."

"No, that's not happening. That can't happen. It's not safe being with me."

Charlotte's eyes flashed down to her tan colored carpet and looked at the bodies now adorned to the floor of her apartment. After seeing what Hall was capable of, she thought he underestimated himself.

"Actually, the safest place right now might be right behind you," she said.

"It's dangerous. I don't know where I'm going, who I'm after, who's after me..."

"OK. So I'll help you figure it out."

Hall let out a deep sigh. Exactly what he didn't want to happen was happening. Charlotte getting mixed up in his problems.

"I don't want you to get involved," Hall said.

"I'm already involved. There's three bodies on my floor."

"But they're not dead."

"I knocked two of them out! Actually, all three! Now they're gonna assume we know each other or friends. You think I can actually stay here and they'll just forgive all that just happened and leave me alone?"

As much as Hall didn't want to accept it, she was right. They were now intertwined by some cruel twist of fate. At least he'd be on the run with someone who wasn't too bad to be around. But maybe that was the problem. Maybe if he was with someone he didn't like, he wouldn't feel so bad if something happened to them. Now he not only had to protect his own life, he had to protect hers. Of course, looking at the floor, maybe she didn't need much protecting. Maybe he should be hiding behind her.

After agreeing to let Charlotte come with her, she quickly grabbed her purse and phone. They then bolted out of the apartment. They ran through the hallway and down the steps, stopping just before they exited the stairwell. Hall opened the door just a tad, enough to see the man with glasses patrolling the apartment entrance.

"You know, I didn't get my keys," Charlotte said.

"Aren't they in your purse?"

"No, I don't usually keep them there. There's a shelf by the TV that I usually keep them on."

"So? What do you need them for?"

"My car?"

"I thought you said you wanted to come with me?"

"I do. But aren't they gonna be looking for your car?"

"Yeah. But they'd be looking for yours too," Hall replied. "You can believe they'll check on it when they wake up."

"Good point. So how are we gonna get past this guy?"

"Guess I can just go up to him and knock him out."

"Does he have a gun?" Charlotte asked.

"Maybe."

"Well, what if he shoots you before you get there?"

"They need me for something. At least they think they do. They won't shoot me until they get what they're looking for. If they were, they'd have done it already."

"Oh. Well what if they decide it's not worth it and just shoot you for the heck of it and then look for their stuff without you?"

Hall just looked at her, thinking she made a good point. He hadn't really thought of that. At some point, they may just think he's too dangerous and not worth the effort anymore. After killing him, they could just look for their stuff on their own and hope they find it. Or if they come to the realization that he really is the wrong man, they may just try to kill him for knowing what was going on. Just before embarking on his plan, Charlotte grabbed his arm to stop him. She felt like she had a better one.

"What if I go out there first?" Charlotte said.

Hall looked at her as if she had two heads. "What? Are you crazy? You can't go out there."

"Why not? This guy doesn't know who I am. He wasn't up there with the others."

Hall looked at the glass wearing man, then back at Charlotte. Her plan certainly made sense, but he still didn't like it. He didn't like potentially putting her in harm's way.

"Just trust me, OK?" Charlotte said.

Hall sighed, still not wanting to go through with it, but reluctantly agreed to let her take the lead. Charlotte exited the stairwell and walked toward the entrance. The glass wearing man saw her approaching but didn't think much of it. She seemed harmless enough. She was walking slowly as if nothing was wrong. Once she got within a few feet of him, she engaged him in conversation.

"Hi," she said.

"Hello."

"Do you live here?"

"Uh, no, no, just waiting for a friend."

Charlotte kept moving, turning to the side to make sure the man's back was turned to Hall, so he could come up behind him and get the jump on him.

"Oh, is your friend a big guy?" Charlotte asked.

"Yeah, that's him. You know him?"

"Sure do. He sent me down here with a message for you."

"Oh yeah? What is it?"

Hall came sneaking down the hallway. He was so quiet the man never heard him coming.

"Uh, he wanted me to tell you about him," Charlotte said, pointing at Hall.

Ricky turned around, only to get a roundhouse kick to the gut. It temporarily took the wind out of him. Hall grabbed him underneath the chin to stand him up straight so he could finish him off.

Ricky knew he was no match for him and was about to get clobbered. He only had one request. "Not the nose! Not the nose!"

Hall didn't pay it much mind, though, and reared back to deliver a powerful punch that landed right on the man's nose. It instantly knocked him down.

"Son of a...," Ricky moaned, holding his face as the pain throttled his nose.

Hall then grabbed Charlotte's hand to hurry up out of the apartment. He didn't see Benny standing just outside though. He effectively had only one arm though and was in no hurry to have his other one broken too. Hall and Charlotte came to an abrupt stop as they saw the shady-looking man standing there. Benny wasn't going to take him on all by himself though. He simply put his good arm up to let Hall know he wasn't putting up a fight.

"I'm not standing in your way," Benny said. Hall just nodded as the two of them rushed past him. As they sprinted toward his car, Benny had some parting words for him. "They're not done with you yet, though. They're gonna keep coming."

6

Hall drove for about twenty minutes without having a destination in mind. He still didn't appear to be thinking clearly as he mostly was concerned about being followed. He seemed to check the rearview mirror every other second.

"I think you can stop checking the mirror now," Charlotte said. "I think it's safe to say they're not behind us."

"Yeah, well, I thought that before I came home too. Look how that turned out."

Hall looked over at Charlotte and observed her fiddling with her fingers as she looked out her window. He felt horrible that she'd gotten mixed up in his business. Even though it really wasn't his fault, he still felt responsible for it. It was obvious that she was nervous and scared with what was happening.

"I guess it's pretty safe to assume now that they're definitely not police," Hall said.

"Yeah, I would say that's a pretty accurate statement."

It was a quiet car ride for the next few minutes as they continued driving. Hall finally broke the silence as he mumbled and grumbled, feeling the pockets on both sides of his pants.

"Crap."

Charlotte looked at him strangely, wondering what his issue was. "You OK over there?"

"Yeah. No. I guess."

"Uh, you wanna say that again?"

"I don't have their wallets anymore," Hall answered. "I guess during one of those battles I must have dropped them or something."

"Do you really need them?"

"No, I guess not. I'm not likely to forget any of their names anytime soon."

Hall then felt the front of his pants, where he last remembered having one of the guns he took from them. That wasn't there either.

"Damn."

Charlotte looked at him again. "What now?"

"I don't have the gun either."

"What gun?"

"Back on the train I took their guns. I had them tucked in my belt."

"And you just realized this now?"

This time, it was Hall's turn to give her a look, feeling like she was giving him a little attitude. "Well excuse me if I was a little busy back there and didn't have time to notice."

"I'm not ragging on you. I just figured a person would know if a gun was missing."

Hall sighed. "I don't even remember when I lost them either. I have a feeling it was when they jumped me in my apartment."

"It doesn't really matter, does it?"

"I suppose not."

"What we really need to do is figure out a plan and what we're doing," Charlotte said. "We can't just drive around the city aimlessly all day."

Hall knew she was right. He just wasn't sure what their next step should be.

"Let's just go to the police and tell them everything."

Hall seemed lukewarm to the idea. "It won't matter much. There's nothing they're gonna be able to do."

"Why not?"

"Even if they go to the apartment, those guys aren't still gonna be there. I still don't know exactly what they want me for, so I can't even tell them that. And without knowing what's going on, they're not gonna be able to give us protection."

"Still, I think it'd still be best if we went there and told them what's going on. At least so they have a record of it and it's on file. In case something happens later."

Hall still thought it would be more of a waste of time, but he relented and started driving toward the police department. Once they got there, and they told their situation to an officer at the front desk, a detective was brought in to get a more formal statement. They were led to an office where they were both questioned, first together, then separately. After being there for an hour, they were beginning to think they were more considered suspects instead of citizens in the wrong place and the wrong time. Charlotte was waiting in another room while Hall was being questioned for a second time.

"So you're telling me that these guys just jumped you on a train, followed you to your apartment, and it's all a case of mistaken identity?" the detective asked, a hint of skepticism in his voice.

Hall threw his hands up in the air and sighed, knowing how strange it all sounded. "That's what I'm telling you."

"It's a little hard to believe, you know. Sounds like it came out of a movie script or something."

"I know that. I'm just telling you what happened. If you don't wanna believe it... OK."

"So those names you gave us... Rex Kowalski, Richard Emmert, and Benjamin Goss... you know who they are?"

"Nope. Never heard of them before today."

"What about the other name you gave us? Palumbo?"

Hall continued shaking his head. "Nope."

"What was his first name?"

"I don't know, he didn't say. Just called him Palumbo."

The detective got up out of his chair and walked around the room a bit. He decided to tell Hall the information he seemed to be missing, finally coming to the conclusion that the man sitting down was telling it to him straight.

"Well since you don't seem to know, I'll clue you in," the detective said. "Ronald Palumbo is a major drug dealer in this area. He's not only into drugs though. Ronnie, as his friends call him, is also into money laundering, stolen jewelry, and half a dozen other offenses. You don't know anything about that?"

"Never even heard of him before today."

"He's a violent and dangerous man. You'd be wise to steer clear of him."

"I would love to. I don't seem to have much of a choice at the moment though."

The detective sat back down to look at Hall face to face. "Look, if this is really on the level, you need to watch out. You're playing with some very dangerous people. They're violent and they don't mind getting rid of people who are standing in their way."

"All I wanted to do was start my own business. I don't know what's going on or why they're after me. Is it possible there was somebody else on the train with the same name as me? Someone who actually is mixed up in all that?"

The detective raised one of his eyebrows and looked at him curiously. "That'd be a mighty tall coincidence, don't you think?"

"Didn't say it wouldn't be. I just don't have any other answers."

"Listen, I'll do a rundown on all the passengers on that train. It's always possible that one of them really was connected, and for whatever reason, they gave Palumbo a false name that'd be carrying the stuff."

"Why would they do that?"

The detective shrugged. "Who knows? Could be a bunch of reasons. It's always possible the real culprit decided to go into business for himself, and then just gave them a name, your name, so they'd be chasing the wrong guy for a while. Then while they're paying attention to you, the other guy slips away without being noticed. It'd be a good scheme if that's what actually happened."

"Is there any way you can tell if that's how it was?"

"It'll take some time, but we'll check out the passenger list and see if any other shady characters were on it."

"Great. So what are we supposed to do in the meantime?"

"If I were you, I'd keep your head low. Because if what you're saying is true, and they think you have their merchandise, whatever it may be, they're gonna keep looking for you."

"I know," Hall said. "Where are we supposed to go though? We can't go back to our apartments, they'll come back looking for us there."

"Friends, family, hotel, somewhere they won't find you."

"Aren't you guys supposed to offer police protection or something?"

"Well there are a few problems with that."

"Such as?"

"One, we don't have the manpower. Two, we don't have the manpower. And three... we don't have the manpower."

"Great."

"Plus, I wouldn't be able to get it approved in your instance, anyway."

"Why not?" Hall asked.

"The circumstances are kind of sketchy."

Hall rolled his eyes and sighed. "Maybe I should just turn the tables on these guys and go after them myself."

The detective tilted his head and pointed at Hall. "Hey, I don't know if you're kidding with that or not. But if you're not, you need to proceed carefully. You do not want to go up against Ronnie Palumbo. Do not get mixed up with that crowd."

"I'm already mixed up with them. What am I supposed to do, just sit down, throw my hands up, and say come and get me? I gotta do something. If you guys can't do it, what else can I do?"

"All I'm gonna say is, whatever you do, make sure it's within the law."

"Oh, I only do things within the law."

After a few more minutes of the question-and-answer session, the detective was finally done with the both of them. Though he wasn't sure he definitely believed it was as simple as Hall laid it out, there was enough doubt in the detective's mind that he thought it could have been possible. There were at least enough red flags to make him check on it, which was better than nothing. Once Hall and Charlotte were cleared to leave, neither of them said a word before getting back in the car. They both seemed a little stunned at what just happened. They just sat there in the car, both with blank expressions on their faces, for several minutes as they stared out the front windshield.

"Was that as uncomfortable for you as it was for me?" Charlotte asked.

"Probably more so."

"I didn't feel like they believed a word I said."

"Well, I guess it's their job to be skeptical. I'm sure they hear a lot of strange stuff."

"Skeptical is one thing. I almost felt like admitting I committed a crime or something just to stop the questions."

Hall snickered, understanding what she meant.

"Well, not to be one of those people that say I told you so..."

"Good. Don't say it."

"But I told you so."

Charlotte whipped her head back and just looked at him. At least they hadn't lost their sense of humor yet, she thought. "What now?"

Hall took a deep breath as he thought. "I dunno. They did tell me that they're all part of a dangerous gang and that they're violent and into a lot of stuff."

"Wonderful. So where does that leave us?"

As Hall brooded over their situation, he finally set aside his reservations about what he knew needed to happen. It was as if a line of thinking to his head just snapped, reeling in a new direction for him. So far, he'd been reacting to everything. If they were both going to survive this ordeal, they were going to have to stop running, barely escaping, narrowly surviving, and start taking the fight to them.

"We need to do something they don't expect," Hall said.

Charlotte wasn't sure she quite liked the sound of that, though she didn't have any idea what it could be. "Which is?"

"Instead of them looking for us, we need to look for them."

"OK," Charlotte said, ready to counter his argument. "That's great and all, and clearly you know how to handle yourself, but uh... this whole fight club thing, isn't really my style. I try to avoid conflict and confrontation, not actively seek it out."

"Listen, they're obviously not gonna stop coming for us. The police can't protect us, we can't hide forever, and eventually they're gonna find us again. I mean, like it or not, that's just the way it is. Unfortunately, we're in the situation we're in, and we're gonna have to find a way out of it. The only way I can think of to do that is to flip the switch. Make them the hunted instead of us."

Charlotte understood what he was saying, and it certainly made sense, but she still had plenty of reservations. "OK, I get all of that, I really do. But... again, I'm not Sly or Arnold, I don't have some major badass gun to go around shooting all over the place, and just in case you forgot, going around and killing people is still.... as far as I know, and correct me if I'm wrong... but it's still kind of illegal, isn't it?"

"First of all, I didn't say we had to go around killing anyone."

"Umm, well, you said yourself, these are violent, dangerous people. What are you going to do? Find out where they live, wake them up in the middle of the night and say, 'Hey, can you please stop coming after me? I'm innocent?' Because clearly, beating them up isn't going to stop them from coming since you've already done it twice, and that guy said plain as day that they were gonna keep coming."

"Boy, you really are a Negative Nancy, aren't ya?"

"It's not being negative, it's being realistic."

"Hey, I didn't ask you to come," Hall said. "I wanted to keep you out of it."

Charlotte's voice started to raise. "You sure have a funny way of doing it, running up to me and barging into my apartment."

"OK, I was trying to protect you."

Charlotte turned and looked out her window, not wanting to argue or lose her cool and say anything dumb. She knew they needed to get along if they were going to get out of this nightmare. Things were hard enough as they were, it wasn't going to get better if they bickered and fought the entire way. Plus, she didn't blame him for her getting involved. It just happened. She knew he was trying to keep her out of it. Maybe it would be different if he seemed like a jerk or something. But he obviously wasn't. He seemed like a good guy too. They both just got thrown into a bad situation and they had to figure out how to deal with it. Together.

Charlotte turned her head back around to look at Hall, who was now staring out his own window, appearing to be just as upset as she was. She tapped his arm to get his attention.

"Hey, I'm sorry, I didn't mean to raise my voice or argue or anything. It's just..."

"I know," Hall replied. "It's just overwhelming. It's not your fault."

"Well it's not your fault either."

"Listen, if there's somewhere you wanna go or someplace you want me to take you, that's fine. I don't mind doing the rest of this alone. I'd actually probably prefer it that way."

Charlotte grinned, appreciating that he was still trying to protect her, but she still felt the same way she did before. "I already told you. The safest place is probably right behind you. We're both in this together now. Let's just do what needs to be done and get it over with."

"OK, well, the first thing we need to do is get as much information as we can to figure out what we're dealing with."

"So what'd you have in mind?"

"Let's find out as much as we can about these guys."

"How do you plan to do that?"

"We need to go somewhere they wouldn't expect," Hall answered.

"Which is where?"

"The library."

Charlotte gave him a confused look. "The library?"

"We need internet, it's as good a spot as any, and I really doubt they'll be looking for us there."

"I hope you're right."

"So do I."

7

Hall and Charlotte spent the next couple of hours at the library, trying to find out as much as they could about their attackers. They looked at newspaper articles, online sources, and public records to learn what they could about Kowalski, Emmert, and Goss, as well as Palumbo. Though Hall initially was doing most of the computer work, with Charlotte sitting next to him and looking over his shoulder, he wasn't getting as far as he wanted to.

"Just out of curiosity, where'd you learn to fight like that?" Charlotte asked.

"I was in the military."

"Oh. What were you in, some kind of special super-power squad or something?"

Hall laughed. "No, just a regular old marine."

"Oh, because it looked like you had a lot of

different moves back there. They train you to do all of that?"

Hall shrugged, not making a big deal of it. "Depends. They train you to do a lot of different things. Some guys take it an extra step."

"I guess you were one of those?"

"I guess."

"Do you mind if I ask another question? It might be kind of bad and I hope you don't get offended or anything."

Hall kept his eyes on the computer as he worked. "So go ahead and ask."

"Could you have killed those guys back there?"

Hall subtly nodded. "I suppose so."

"I kind of had a feeling you could have, considering your training and all. I guess I'm asking because... well, if you could have, why didn't you? Not that I'm advocating for killing anyone or anything. It just crossed my mind."

"I guess the best reason I can come up with is that I just don't want to kill anyone anymore."

"Anymore? You killed people before?"

A lump went down Hall's throat before answering. "Yes."

"How many?"

"I don't know. I didn't stop to count them."

"While you were in the service, I take it?"

"Yeah. I did several tours in Afghanistan, Iraq, not to mention a few other places I can't talk about."

"You think you could kill again if you had to?" Charlotte asked.

Hall stopped his typing and looked at her. "I guess so. Why all the questions about this?"

"Like you said, we're dealing with dangerous people who may try to do that to us. I just want to be prepared."

"And you're wondering if it came down to their lives or ours whether I'm willing to do what's necessary?"

Charlotte just shrugged as she looked down at the ground. Suddenly she felt kind of embarrassed to talk about it. She felt like maybe she had stepped over the line in talking to him about it. Hall wasn't upset with the line of questioning though. She was knee-deep in this now too. He brought her into this and she had every right to inquire about anything she deemed worthy enough to ensure her survival. He gently put his hand on top of hers, which was resting on her knee. She lifted her head up to look him in the eye.

"If it comes down to it, and it's their life or yours, I won't hesitate to do what has to be done."

Charlotte let out a smile as Hall did the same. He then turned back to the computer and started working again.

"You know, I never did ask you what you do for a living."

"Oh, I work with computers," Charlotte replied.

"Yeah? Doing what?"

"Mostly design work. I work part time for an advertising company helping them with stuff, then I also have my own business that I do on the side. I design websites, marketing materials, entertainment stuff, all kinds of things."

"Sounds interesting. I take it you're not gonna get fired from anything in the next couple of days if you stay out of sight?"

"No, I should be good."

As soon as the words left her mouth, Charlotte turned her head slightly, as if something else had entered her mind. Right after Hall said it might take a couple days to figure everything out, her mind started racing. Where were they going to go? Where would they sleep? It was the first time that she actually thought of the situation dragging on for more than the day they were in. It was a scary thought to think that this might drag on for a while. She didn't know if she could do this for more than a day or two.

Hall just happened to glance over at her and noticed the panic-stricken look on her face. He wondered what was going through her mind now. He stopped typing and turned towards her again.

"What's wrong?"

"Oh. It's, uh, it's nothing."

"Don't give me that," Hall replied. "We're tied at the hip now. No secrets or holding things back."

She was almost too embarrassed to say. "It's just our, um, sleeping arrangement I guess."

After not getting it at first, it then finally sank in for Hall. "Oh. I understand." Considering he'd slept in every kind of place imaginable, he wasn't that picky about where he slept anymore. He could probably make himself comfortable sleeping in a bathtub or a closet if he had to. But he was sympathetic to her concerns. "Listen, it's just for a couple of days till we get all this figured out. I don't think it'd be a good idea if we split up, even while we're sleeping."

"Yeah, you're probably right."

Though she didn't seem as concerned as she was, Hall still thought he detected a hint of worry. "It's nothing to be worried about. Wherever we go, I can sleep on the floor, or a bathroom, wherever. You don't have to worry about me or anything."

Charlotte smiled and nodded. "I think there's a vending machine outside. You want a soda or something?"

"Yeah, sure. Thanks."

"OK. I'll be right back."

As she got up, Hall turned and watched her leave. He thought back to her questions about whether he could kill again if he had to. He started beating himself over his reluctance to kill his attackers already. He certainly could have done it on the train if he wanted to. And he had the chance again at both of their apartments. He just had trouble making that final call to end their lives.

But as he watched Charlotte go out the front door

of the library, he couldn't help but think it was all his fault she was here. Part of him felt like he was just postponing the inevitable. Maybe she was right. If he was going to go after them, how was he going to finish the fight? He couldn't just keep knocking them down, only to have to deal with them again once they got back up. It was never going to end that way. He was going to have to get mean. He was going to have to get violent. Even more so than he had been. If he had done that to begin with, Charlotte wouldn't have to worry about this mess. If he'd just finished the three men off on the train, maybe the whole thing would already be over with.

Once Charlotte came back into the library, her eyes immediately locked onto Hall's. But he didn't seem to really be there. Though he was looking at her direction, it seemed as if he was looking right through her. He obviously had something else on his mind. She came right up to him and he didn't even notice her presence. After holding his soda out for a minute, Charlotte finally tapped him on the shoulder with it.

"Huh?" he said, the touch of the plastic bottle waking him from his gaze.

Charlotte sat back down. "So what's on your mind?"

"Ahh, it's nothing."

"Hey, weren't you the one just a few minutes ago saying no secrets?"

"Using my words against me already?"

"If the shoe fits. You were obviously thinking about something. Might as well spill it."

Hall took a sip of his soda first, deliberating whether he wanted to say. But he couldn't think of anything else, and she was right in using his own words against him. They shouldn't have any secrets. "I was just thinking about how you were right."

"In regards to?"

"Killing them."

"What do you mean?"

"I should've done it when we were on the train," Hall replied. "I could've. They were down. I had them. If I had, maybe this would already be over with. Maybe you wouldn't have to worry about where you'll be in five hours."

Charlotte could tell by the way he was hanging his head that he felt bad about her getting involved. Once again she tried to persuade him that it wasn't his fault. "You can't go around kicking yourself over things that are in the past. Things happen and they happen fast. This isn't a video game where you get to retry or have a do-over. You had your reasons for doing whatever you did. Just gotta move on from it. Now you have to live in the present, not the past."

Hall picked his head up, feeling a little more encouraged. "You know, if your career as a graphic designer doesn't pan out, you could always become a motivational speaker."

"Ew, no way."

"Why not?"

"I don't like talking in front of people. I'm a pretty quiet and reserved person."

Hall and Charlotte stared at each other for a few moments in between sips of their sodas. In one of their earlier encounters in the hallway, before all this went down, Hall had thought about having a moment like this with her. He had contemplated inviting her out for a drink, and having some quiet time together to get to know each other, though having a soda together in the library wasn't exactly what he had in mind. After stopping their gaze, Hall turned back to the computer.

"So, you having much luck with that?" Charlotte asked.

"Haven't you been watching?"

"Only vaguely. I haven't been looking at every single thing you've done."

Hall seemed frustrated and let out a sigh, though it wasn't directed at her. "Feels like I'm kind of hitting a dead end."

"How do you mean?"

Hall started flailing his hands around above the keyboard to help demonstrate his irritation. "I'm looking for something other than the obvious. I mean, I know their names, I know they're bad guys, I've seen some stories about them, things like that, but I'm looking for something deeper. Something we can really use against them."

"You mean where they have vacation homes at,

who their girlfriends are, where they get their cars washed, things like that?"

"Yeah, I guess that's it."

Charlotte gave him a wry smile, then put her hand on his arm to gently and playfully push him to the side. "Move over."

"What are you gonna do?"

"I'm gonna find out what you want."

"How are you gonna do that?" Hall asked.

Charlotte gave him a perky look as if she should be offended for even being asked such a question. "Please, this is child's play. Leave this to the pro's."

"Which is you, I take it?"

"Man, I've been messing around with computers since I was eleven years old. I built my own computer when I was fifteen. Finding information about people on the internet is easy. It's just a matter of know-how."

"And you know how?"

"Sure do," Charlotte answered, flashing him a teasing smile.

"Well why didn't you say so before?"

"You didn't ask."

"So you just let me goof around on here for the last two hours without offering to help?" Charlotte didn't reply and again tantalized him with her smile. "Glad someone hasn't lost their sense of humor."

8

It wasn't long before Charlotte found some interesting material on their targets. She found much more than Hall did. She printed out a couple pages of notes, most of which were centered on Palumbo and Kowalski. The other two were not as easily found, mostly because they were not as high up on the ladder. Palumbo and Kowalski were the two main guys. They made the decisions. They were the ones Hall and Charlotte needed to target. If they were out of the way, the others would follow their lead. The others were just there for muscle.

Hall grabbed the printout and placed it on the counter so they both could look at it. Charlotte had found multiple things of interest on both Palumbo and Kowalski. They each owned several businesses that they could visit, including a nightclub that Kowalski owned, which would be their first target.

Hall ran his finger over some of the information on the paper as he read it. When he finished, he brought it back up to the name of the nightclub. "That's it. That's where we go first."

"Why there?"

"For one, there will probably be a lot of people, so we should be able to blend in. Second, they won't be expecting us."

"But you don't even know if they're going to be there," Charlotte said. "They might be out looking for us or they might be in half a dozen other places."

Hall didn't seem to care. "Gotta start somewhere right?"

They finished up at the library, then went to their car. They still had some time to kill before the club opened. Hall didn't want to just aimlessly drive around the city for a couple of hours, figuring the more they were out and about, the more likely they were to be found. They eventually decided on dinner, hoping to spend an hour or two at a diner or a fast-food joint.

Their plan was basically to go to whatever food place they found first, wherever it might have been. After a few minutes of driving, they stopped at a fast-food restaurant. They sat there for about two hours, just talking and eating, getting to know each other better. As they talked, they almost seemed to forget all the trouble they were in, focusing on each other instead of the things they'd been through, and the things they still had yet to do. It was nice to actually forget their troubles for a little while.

"I think we met, what, three times before this?" Charlotte asked.

"Yeah, I think that's right."

"I'd always pegged you for an ex-military guy."

"Oh yeah? Why's that?"

"I think it's the haircut. It's a dead giveaway."

Hall smiled. "Maybe I'll have to change my look. Maybe I'll grow my hair long, have a ponytail or something."

"Ew, no."

"Don't think I could pull that look off?" Hall asked.

"No, I don't think so. I think you look good just the way you are."

As soon as she said it, she batted her eyes quickly, realizing she was coming off as being flirty. She looked away and sipped her soda through the straw. Hall didn't really give her comment much thought as he took a bite of his cheeseburger. As he chewed, and Charlotte's face was turned to the side, he couldn't help but think how pretty she looked. It probably wasn't the time or place for that, but he wished they were there under different circumstances.

"You wanna hear something funny?" Hall asked.

"I could probably use a laugh."

"I was, uh, thinking about asking you out on a date the next time I saw you."

A big smile came across Charlotte's face, not having any idea that he was into her. "You were?"

"Yeah. Kinda funny now that I think about it."

"What's so funny about it?"

"Well, assuming you would have accepted my invitation, I had thought about taking you out to dinner somewhere to get to know each other better. It was kind of nerve-wracking, thinking of what to say, what you'd say, you know, all that. And now here we are. Turns out I didn't have to do any of that. I just had to push you back into your apartment and put your life in danger."

The two let out a laugh, somehow finding humor in the situation. They went back to eating their food for another minute or two, both thinking about things. Charlotte then broke the silence.

"You know, I probably would have said yes."

Hall stopped chewing midstream as his eyes darted back up at her. A slight smile shined through as he finished eating. "Only probably?"

"Yeah. Probably."

"That's all you're gonna give me?"

"For now," Charlotte replied, finding some joy in teasing him.

Not long after finishing their food, Charlotte's phone rang. She picked it up, and it was her father. They often talked, so she didn't think anything of it at the time.

"Hey, Dad."

"Hey, is everything OK?"

Charlotte scrunched her eyebrows together, not sure what he was referring to. "Yeah, everything's fine, why?"

"I just had a police officer knocking on the door asking questions about you."

"What? A police officer?"

"Yeah. They said you were in some kind of trouble and they were looking for you. They wanted to know where you might have gone because you had left your apartment. What's going on?"

"Nothing's going on, everything's fine," Charlotte answered, having a good idea as to who knocked on her father's door.

"Then why are they looking for you?"

"It was just a mistake. Everything's fine now. Promise."

"Are you lying to me? I mean, I can't help you if you don't tell me what's going on."

"Dad, everything's fine. What was the name of the guy you talked to?"

"Uh, I don't remember exactly. A Detective Kow... Kowals... Kowl... I don't know, something like that."

"Big guy?"

"Yeah. You know him?"

Charlotte didn't want her father knowing what was really going on, so she wasn't going to tell him the truth, so she had to figure out a way to set his mind at ease. She quickly thought of something.

"Yeah, yeah, I already talked to him. Everything's good now."

"Well what was the problem?"

"It was someone I was doing design work for. They were looking for him and they wanted to see if I knew anything about him."

"Oh. So it's nothing about you?"

"Of course not," Charlotte replied. "What would I have done?"

"I don't know. That's why I was checking. He made it sound like you'd done something wrong."

"No, don't be silly. See? Do I sound upset or worried?"

"No."

"So obviously nothing's wrong. I must have talked to that detective just after he contacted you, so everything's cleared up already."

"OK, good."

"What else did he say?"

"Not much. Just wanted to know if I knew where you were. I think he didn't quite believe me at first when I said I didn't know, but he left after a few minutes."

"He say anything else?" Charlotte asked, getting worried.

"No, not really."

As soon as Charlotte hung up, she tossed the phone down on the table, and the pleasant expression on her face faded into an angry death stare. She was immediately worried about her family, hoping the men didn't go from one family member to another in order to find her.

Hall was intently listening to her conversation and had already figured out what she was discussing based on the words that he was picking up.

"What's wrong?"

His question got no response, and it didn't seem like Charlotte even heard him. Her head was down and her eyes were dancing around the table, thinking of all the things that could happen. Hall tried talking to her again, but she was so deep in thought that she wasn't hearing a word he was saying.

"What's the matter?" Hall asked.

After getting no response this time, Hall reached his hand across the table and slipped it into hers. The touch of his hand awoke her from her trance. Feeling his hand, she gripped it a little tighter and looked into his eyes, though she still didn't say anything.

"What's wrong?" Hall asked again.

Charlotte took a big gulp and took a few seconds to collect herself and her thoughts. "Kowalski showed up at my parents' house and talked to my dad. Told him he was a detective. Probably flashed him the fake badge that he showed me."

"Is he OK?"

"Yeah, he's fine. I'm just hoping they don't do anything to my family or use them to try and get to us."

"I don't think you have to worry about that," Hall said, still holding her hand.

"Why not?"

Hall shrugged. "What good would it do?"

"Because they're my family and I don't want anything to happen to them."

"No, I don't mean that. I mean, what good would it do Kowalski to hurt them? Wouldn't get them anywhere."

"Oh. Well what if they try to kidnap them or something to draw us out?"

"How would they contact us to let us know? You gotta look at it from their standpoint. Hurting them wouldn't do them any good, it'd only make us go into hiding even more. And if they think we're staying away from friends or family, then it wouldn't make sense to bring even more people into this. It'd only give them more of a headache."

Charlotte rubbed his hand with her thumb, his words making her feel slightly better. She wasn't entirely sure she believed everything he was saying or whether he was just saying it to get her mind off of it, but in either case, his words were comforting to hear. They sat there quietly together, neither one feeling uncomfortable or out-of-place holding each other's hand. After another minute, they finally released each other's grip.

Though they were both obviously interested in each other, they were wary of getting too close, too attached to the other. They both knew of situations where people got close to someone else because of a certain situation they were in. Neither wanted to get close to the other, only to find out after this predicament was over, that one of their feelings had waned. Besides, they had more important things to do at the moment. Falling for each other would be worthless if they weren't alive at the end of it to see it through.

"You wanna head out soon?" Hall asked.

"Sure. Where to?"

"Might as well head to the club."

Charlotte looked at the time, knowing it still didn't open for a few hours yet. "Already? Kinda early, isn't it? Doesn't open for two or three hours."

"Yeah, but if we get there soon, maybe we can see who goes in. Scout around a little bit. If there's one thing my military training taught me... is you always scout out your enemy first."

9

Once Hall and Charlotte arrived at The Mix, the nightclub legally owned by Kowalski, there weren't many cars in the parking lot. Probably only half a dozen or so. They still had a few hours before the club opened, so they figured it was unlikely any of their targets would be there yet. They assumed it was mostly workers getting the place ready.

Just to be sure, though, they drove through the lot to get a read on the license plates of the cars that were there. Through Charlotte's excellent computer work, they were able to get the plate number of the car that Kowalski was supposed to be driving. They compared the number they had with the rest of the cars, but there wasn't a match. With so few cars there yet, they didn't want to stay and risk being spotted, so they drove out of the lot, going to a nearby shopping center that was only down the street. With their new positioning, they could still see the entrance to the club and would be able to see if the make of Kowalski's car pulled in.

An hour went by, and several more cars made their way into the parking lot. None of which matched Kowalski's though. It did afford Hall and Charlotte more time to talk and get to know each other.

"So what exactly is your plan once you get in there?" Charlotte asked. "Assuming that Kowalski does show up, that is?"

"I'll give him one more chance to back off."

"And if he doesn't?"

"Then I guess whatever happens after that is on him," Hall replied.

Though Charlotte didn't outwardly disagree, she did believe it was a waste of time. "He's not going to believe you."

"Like I said, all I can do is try."

Charlotte looked out her window and slightly shook her head. "And what are we going to do if he doesn't show up? We don't even know if he's here that much. Just because he owns the place, doesn't mean he's actively involved in the business."

"Just a hunch. After everything that's gone down today, he might wanna unwind, try to get in a better mood."

"You know they're gonna have security around, not to mention those other guys he's been with."

"Yeah."

"What if they have cameras hooked up and see you come in?" Charlotte asked.

"They do. I saw a couple on the outside of the building when we drove through the parking lot. One's pointed at the door."

"So don't you think we should try to not be so noticeable if we go inside?"

"How you wanna do that?"

Charlotte turned around and looked at the stores that were behind them. She saw a clothing store that should do the trick. She grabbed her purse and opened the door.

"I'll be back in a few minutes," she said. "Don't go anywhere without me."

"Wouldn't dream of it. Where are you going?"

"Shopping."

Hall watched her leave through his rear-view and side mirrors. He watched her walk into a clothing store and assumed she was getting some type of disguise. In the time she was gone, a few more cars pulled into the club's lot, but still not the car he was hoping to see. Charlotte was only gone about ten minutes. Hall saw her coming back through his mirror, holding a white-colored shopping bag.

"Get anything good?" Hall asked.

"I sense a bit of sarcasm?"

"Not at all."

Charlotte opened the bag and removed a couple of

hats and two pairs of sunglasses. She passed one of each to her partner.

"What are these?" Hall asked.

"It's called a hat and sunglasses."

Hall tried not to crack a smile as he tried the sunglasses on. "Yes, I know. Why do we need these?"

"So we aren't spotted when we go inside. Duh. Haven't you seen any spy movies?"

"This stuff only works in the movies," Hall said, putting the hat and sunglasses to the side.

"If we both put on the hat and sunglasses, if Kowalski does happen to be there, and we slip in with a bunch of other people who are also going in at the same time, he won't recognize us."

"Sure of that?"

"Yes. We'll just be another guy and girl going into the club for a good time."

"With a hat and sunglasses."

"We live in California, everyone has sunglasses."

"What's with all this we stuff?" Hall asked. "You're not going in."

"Why not?"

"It's too dangerous."

"Excuse me, who knocked out all three of those guys in my apartment?"

"Listen, you got in some lucky shots because they weren't expecting you to hurt them."

"Oh, what, because I'm a woman I can't be dangerous?"

"I didn't say that," Hall answered, sensing he got himself into trouble.

"Well that's what you're implying."

Hall put his hands up, tapping them on the steering wheel, trying to figure out how to get himself out of the deep end. He certainly wasn't trying to offend her and knew he put his foot in his mouth.

"Look, you're obviously very capable of defending yourself. There's no doubt of that. All I'm trying to say is that... I don't know what we might be running into in there. I'd feel a lot better if you were on the outside."

"Safe and sound and all that?"

"Why do you wanna keep sticking your nose into things?"

"Because my nose is as deep into this as yours is now," Charlotte replied. "And besides, how many times do I have to tell you, the safest place is right behind you?"

"The safest place will actually be in the car. If I get into it hot and heavy and have to run out of there, you can be ready to whisk me away."

"I think it'd be better if I was in there with you watching your back."

Hall huffed and puffed, sensing he wasn't going to get his way. "You know, you're more stubborn than I assumed you were."

Charlotte just shrugged, not really caring. "Oh well." Hall stopped arguing, figuring he wasn't going to win. Charlotte was surprised that he gave up so easily, not that she was going to give in. “Is that it?”

“Is what it?”

“You’re not going to keep fighting about it?”

“I figure it’s not gonna do any good, so why bother?”

“Oh.”

“I mean, I could just go in without you and tell you to stay in the car, but somehow I get the feeling you might not listen.”

“What gives you that impression?” Charlotte asked with a devious smile.

“Just a hunch.”

They waited in the same spot for several more hours. They watched car after car go into the lot, none of which was what they were hoping for. The club had opened, and the parking lot was now getting pretty tight.

“Guess it’s a popular spot,” Hall said.

“Yeah, usually is.”

Hall slowly turned his head and looked at his passenger. “You come here often?”

Charlotte almost hated to admit that she’d been there before. “Yeah, a couple times.”

“Didn’t you tell me these places weren’t your type of scene?”

“They’re not. I got dragged here by my friends so I agreed to come along. This would never be my first choice to go.”

"Oh, dragged here by your friends," Hall said, sounding like he didn't believe her. "I see."

"I did!"

"Right."

"Hey!"

Hall let out a laugh to let her know he was joking. Charlotte's blood was starting to boil, but she quickly calmed down and laughed too.

"I was thinking..."

"Stop that," Hall kidded.

"No, really, I was thinking..."

"I told you not to do that."

"Would you stop joking around and listen to me?"

Hall wiped the smile on his face and restrained himself from any further quips. "OK, go ahead."

"I take it you've never been in there?"

"Good assumption."

"Since I have, I already know the layout in there."

"Maybe they've changed it," Hall replied. "When was the last time you were there?"

"Unfortunately, about a month ago."

"Oh. Why do you say unfortunately?"

"Because I hated it. Three guys tried hitting on me."

"Isn't that the idea?"

"Maybe for some people," Charlotte answered. "Not for me though."

"You go out with any of them?"

"No! I told you I don't like this scene. Anyway, can

you stop asking me these questions so we can get back to my plan?"

"I was trying to avoid it."

"I figured as much. Since I know the layout, we can go in together like we're a couple, then eventually make our way to where the offices are."

"Which you obviously know where they are?"

"Yep," Charlotte proudly said. "Once you go in, there's a little entrance area, then the bar to the left, the main floor to the center, then to the right are a bunch of tables and seats and stuff. Then further to the right past the tables is a long hallway that leads to bathrooms and stuff like that."

"OK? So where's the offices?"

"In the hallway to the bathrooms, there's a staircase that goes to the second floor. Says authorized personnel only, so I assume that's where the offices are."

"Is there a guard standing there?"

"No, it's just a door."

"Then how do you know there's steps there?"

"Because the one time I was walking to the bathroom, one of the employees opened the door as I walked past. I looked over and saw the steps. What do you think, I'm just making it up?"

"I'm just asking how you knew."

They were just about to continue their lively discussion when they suddenly stopped. Hall's eyes opened wide as he saw a car that looked like Kowalski's drive by. He couldn't get the plate number, but he just got the feeling that it was his.

"I think that's it," Hall excitedly said.

"Are you sure?"

"No, but I just got a hunch that it is."

Hall quickly turned the car on and was about to leave before Charlotte pumped the brakes for him. She put her hand on his arm to slow him down.

"Slow down there, cowboy."

"What?" Hall asked, wanting to get going.

"Let him get in and get situated first... if that's actually him."

"Why do that?"

"What are you gonna do, have a fight in the parking lot? A lot of witnesses and other people around. I assumed you wanted to get him alone."

Hall sighed, realizing she was right. "Yeah."

"Besides, you don't even know if it's him. Just wait a few minutes, then we can pull in and see if the license plates match." Hall nodded, agreeing to her request. "It might take him some time to get to his office, anyway. Maybe he greets employees on the way or something."

"I don't wanna wait an hour."

"We don't have to. Let's give it about twenty minutes."

"I'll give him ten."

"Fifteen."

Hall looked at her and sighed again. "Fine. Fifteen." He immediately looked at his watch to start the countdown. "Why does it seem like you're always getting your way with things?"

"Because I'm a woman and I know what I'm talking about."

"What are you saying? I don't know what I'm talking about?"

"I'm saying you're a little overeager to finish this and could rush into things and make a mistake. Men don't always think with their heads sometimes... at least not the one on their shoulders."

Hall just glared at her, though he couldn't deny that she may have been right. He was a little overzealous to get this ordeal over with. He needed to slow down, think things through clearly before acting on them. He patiently tried to wait the next fifteen minutes, though he was a little fidgety thinking about what he had to do. He tapped the steering wheel with the tips of his fingers for most of the time. Charlotte could tell he was anxious, and the constant tapping didn't really bother her. Whatever worked for him to calm his nerves, she thought. After the fifteen minutes was up, Hall looked over at his partner, ready to get moving.

"Are you ready to go now?" Hall facetiously asked.

"Don't get sarcastic."

"You sure you wanna do this and go in with me? You don't have to, you know."

"I told you. I'm going where you go."

"OK. Be ready for anything."

10

Once Hall parked the car, he gave Charlotte another look. She put her hat and sunglasses on and waited for him. He gave her an eye roll, then reached down for his hat and put it on as well. He drew the line at the sunglasses though. The sun had already set down for the night and he wasn't going to be one of those people who wore them at all hours of the night.

"OK, let's just get this out in the open," Hall said, picking up the sunglasses. "This is ridiculous. The hat I can understand. That's fine. But I'm not wearing these." He tossed the sunglasses back down on the dashboard.

"What's the matter with them?"

"In case you haven't noticed... it's nighttime. It'd be fine if it was twelve o'clock in the afternoon. But it isn't. The sun went down an hour ago. I'm not going to imitate the song."

"What song?"

"Never mind, I'm not going to sing it. And I'm not going to wear them. And you're not either."

Charlotte took the shades off and looked out the window, feeling like he had a pretty good point. The whole idea was to get in undetected, and anyone wearing sunglasses at night, would likely stick out like a sore thumb. She capitulated to his request and put them aside.

"You don't happen to remember if they had cameras inside, do you?" Hall asked.

"No. You may find this hard to believe but I've never noticed them or tried to look for them before meeting you."

Hall just gave her a look without saying anything. The two then got out of the car and started walking toward the entrance of the club. Almost in unison, they both pulled their hats down a little, preventing most of their face from being seen by the outside cameras. As a large group of people walked toward the front door, Hall and Charlotte slid in amongst them, right in the middle. Charlotte slipped her arm around Hall's, interlocking their elbows. She cozied up to his arm to make it seem like they were a real couple.

As the line stalled to get into the building, with their arms embraced, Charlotte tilted her head to rest it on Hall's shoulder. Though Hall thought she might have been laying it on a little thick, not thinking she had to go that far to sell it that they were just like a normal couple, he really didn't mind it. It was actually kind of nice, he thought. It'd been a long time since he'd been with a girl. The last girlfriend he had was back in high school. He enlisted in the army soon after graduating and had been in the service ever since. Though he had a fling or two over the years, up until that moment, it never occurred to him how much he missed the touch of a woman. He hoped that they would make it through this mess so he could one day have it again.

As Charlotte's head rested upon Hall's shoulder, she also thought she might have been overdoing it. But since she'd already done it, she didn't want to just yank it away. Plus Hall didn't seem to mind, so she just kept up with it. For a brief moment, she'd almost forgotten about all the trouble they'd gotten into.

It'd been about two years since she broke up with her last boyfriend. Ever since she discovered that he'd been cheating on her, she dumped him and had been on her own. Though her friends had always been encouraging her to go out and meet someone, she was content with her life. But she had to admit to herself, that it felt nice to actually be with someone again. Even if it was only for a few seconds.

As soon as the two of them finally got inside the club, they let go of each other. They took a quick look around to see if they saw Kowalski, or any of his friends. They didn't immediately notice him, so they went to the bar and ordered drinks. With their drinks in hand, they went over and found a table.

Once they sat down, Hall picked up his drink and held it in front of his face like he was about to drink it. He turned his head slightly in each direction as his eyes glanced up to the edges of the walls as they met the ceiling, looking for security cameras. He saw a few, though none were pointed at the table they were at.

"When are we gonna make our move?" Charlotte asked.

"Weren't you the one who told me to be more patient?"

"Yeah, but that was before we got in here. Now I wanna hurry up and get out of here."

Charlotte's nerves were starting to get the better of her. Though she mustered up enough courage to go in there, it now wasn't sounding like such a good idea. Back at the apartment, everything happened so fast, and she didn't have much of a choice. She was involved before she even knew what hit her. And then joining him just seemed like the right idea. But now, she was willfully putting herself into a potentially violent situation.

"We'll wait a few more minutes," Hall said. "I wanna make sure he's actually there. Last thing we need is to go break into his office only to find out he's not there and he's really out here somewhere."

Charlotte started sipping on her drink to calm her nerves. Hall could tell she was anxious. Her hands looked like they were shaking a little. She was eagerly looking all around when Hall put his hand on top of hers to calm her down. She was startled a little, but Hall gently squeezed her hand.

"Just relax," Hall said. "Everything will be alright."

Charlotte looked at him and gave him a smile. As the two locked eyes for a moment, she really believed that it would be. There was a warmth and gentleness to his voice that made her think he was right. As they held hands for a minute, Charlotte's heart rate started slowing down, finally getting a grip on her nerves. They continued holding hands for a few minutes, just like they were any other couple. Finally, Hall released her hand, causing Charlotte to look over at him, wondering if something was wrong. By the look on his face, something was.

"What is it?" Charlotte asked.

Hall nodded toward the bar. "He's over there. Kowalski."

Charlotte immediately snapped her head in that direction. She didn't quite see him at first with all the people walking by getting in her way. Once some of the people cleared, she picked him up. The black eye he was now sporting instantly stuck out at her.

"Jeez, you really did a number on him, didn't you?" Charlotte asked. "Look at that eye. Looks like he just went twelve rounds with Mike Tyson or something."

"You know Mike Tyson?"

"Yeah, I'm not dumb. My dad used to watch replays

of old boxing matches. Sometimes I'd watch with him."

Hall was impressed. He was also a fan of boxing and mixed martial art contests. He never thought he'd run into a woman who was as well. "So who was better, Ali or Frazier?"

"Ali of course."

Hall shook his head, still keeping his eyes firmly on Kowalski at the bar. "No, definitely Frazier."

"You're definitely out of your mind. Ali won two of their three bouts. He obviously was better on the basis of winning the series."

Hall was about to continue the argument when he saw Kowalski leaving the bar. The two of them put their heads down and fumbled around with their drinks as Kowalski walked by them. He was followed by one of his stooges, the one with the broken arm, which was now in a sling. Hall, keeping his head down, slowly turned around to see the two men walking down the hallway that Charlotte said led to the bathrooms and offices.

"And by the way, how do you know it was me that did it to his face?" Hall asked. "Maybe it was you with that frying pan."

"Oh. Good point. Guess we can take credit fifty-fifty."

"We gonna go now?"

"In a minute. Let them get settled in first."

"OK."

"What about UFC?" Hall asked. "Best fighter all time? Liddell or Couture?"

"Neither."

"What?"

"It's obviously Anderson Silva."

"What?!" Hall demonstratively asked. "What? There's no way."

"Listen, your guys are good fighters, but they just wouldn't win a match against him."

"In their primes, Couture would mop the floor with him."

Charlotte rolled her eyes. "OK, you're just embarrassing yourself now. We need to go before you completely humiliate yourself."

Hall stopped their conversation, figuring he didn't have enough time to sway her mind to come around to his line of thinking. But he definitely was going to remember this discussion for another time. They waited a few more minutes before leaving the table, finishing their drinks first. Before getting up, Hall made sure that Charlotte was ready.

"You can still wait in the car."

Charlotte forcefully pushed her empty glass across the table. "Let's go."

The two got up and moved away from the table, walking down the hallway.

"We'll each head into the bathroom for a minute," Hall said.

They walked past the door that led to the upstairs

offices. Passing a few other customers on the way, they each went into their respective bathrooms for a minute. Upon going in, Charlotte headed for a sink and splashed a little water on her face. Her nerves were starting to come back. After putting some water on her face, she looked in the mirror, asking herself how she got here. Knowing that Hall was probably outside waiting for her already, she hurried up and dried herself off. Once she came out of the bathroom, she saw Hall leaning up against the wall.

"You OK?" Hall asked.

"Just fine."

They moved back down the hall, stopping as they got to the door that led upstairs. Hall put his hand on the handle of the door and tried to open it, but it wouldn't budge.

"It's locked," Hall whispered.

They stood there for a moment, waiting for some people to pass by. They looked at each other, neither knowing what to do next.

"Can't you do something... or something?" Charlotte asked.

"Like what?"

"I dunno, pick the lock or something."

"I don't know how to pick a lock," Hall replied.

"You were in the army."

"So?"

"So don't they teach you how to do stuff like that."

"No, they teach you how to kick it in or blow it up."

"Oh. Guess that wouldn't work here."

"I would say not."

A minute later, their questions were answered. The door opened up, with an average size, middle-aged man stepping out. Before the door closed, Hall reached out and grabbed the edge of it. He looked on the other side of it, but no one was there. He took another look back and nodded at Charlotte to follow him. They slowly walked up the carpeted steps, almost expecting to run into someone. They didn't though, and walked straight up the steps unimpeded, leading to another small hallway. There were two doors on each side of the hall.

"Kinda surprised they don't have a guard or something out here," Charlotte said softly.

No sooner than the words left her mouth, one of the doors opened, the one directly to their right, and a rather large muscular man stepped out.

"Hey, what are you guys doing up here? No one's allowed up here."

Hall had to think quickly. "Oh, uh, I had an interview scheduled with Mr. Kowalski."

The man looked at Hall strangely, not sure if he believed the story. He was usually informed of any unauthorized personnel showing up. But he wasn't told anything about an interview taking place.

"Nobody said anything about an interview."

"Just ask Mr. Kowalski," Hall said. "He'll verify it."

"Who's she?"

"She's also applying for a position. We were both told to come here by a mutual friend of Mr. Kowalski's, so he said he'd talk to us both at once since he was pretty busy."

The man stood there for a second, analyzing their faces. It didn't seem like they were trying to put one over on him, he thought.

"Wait here, I'll see if he's ready."

The man turned and walked down the hall until he got to the door on the far left. Just before he knocked, Hall spoke up, not wanting Kowalski to be alerted he was there yet.

"Oh, you know what," Hall said, walking down to the man's position. Charlotte followed him. "I think our interview was supposed to be tomorrow."

The large man appeared to be extremely displeased, thinking his time was being wasted. Hall turned to get a confirmation from Charlotte on the time.

"Wasn't it supposed to be tomorrow?" Hall asked. "Or was it today?"

"No, I think you're right," she replied. "It was definitely tomorrow. Yeah. Tomorrow."

Hall looked at the man with almost a comical look, shrugging and nodding at the same time. "Sorry."

The man put his hand on Hall's shoulder, ready to escort them out of the building. "You guys need to get out of here."

Hall turned his back to the man, seemingly ready

to comply with his wishes. Sensing no trouble, the man was surprised when Hall suddenly turned around. Hall grabbed hold of the man's wrist, twisted it, then applied a great amount of force to get him to the ground. Hall switched positions, getting onto the man's back as he pushed up on the man's arm. With Charlotte watching, a painful expression came onto her face. It almost hurt just watching Hall punish the man. With the man screaming in pain, Hall applied more force, tearing the muscles in the man's shoulders, along with possibly breaking his elbow. Charlotte turned away for a second and covered her mouth, not wanting to watch anymore.

Satisfied that the man was neutralized, Hall got up and started walking back to Kowalski's office. As he was about to enter, he took a quick look back to make sure Charlotte was right behind him, but she wasn't there. He then saw her kneeling down by the large man that he just took out. She reached inside his sport jacket and removed a gun, holding it by the handle with her fingers and turning away from it like she was holding a dead animal or something.

"What are you doing?" Hall whispered.

Charlotte just stuck her hand out so he could take the gun from her. "I don't know. I thought you might need this."

"Good thinking."

"You really like doing that, huh?" Charlotte asked.

"What's that?"

"Breaking people's arms. Seems to be a habit with you."

"Well it was either that or kill him," Hall said. "Seems to be the best way to take someone out without sending them to the cemetery. Better to have a broken arm than be dead. Isn't it?"

"Umm, yeah, I guess so."

As they stood there by the door, Hall was slightly surprised that nobody else heard the man scream and came running out. Maybe it was a regular occurrence, he thought. In any case, he took one last look at the man on the floor, who still seemed to be in quite a bit of agony, lying on the floor and holding his arm and shoulder.

Hall put his hand on the handle of the door and tried to open it, but it was locked. He made a thrusting motion with his head, obviously displeased he couldn't just barge right in and get the drop on whoever was in there. He grabbed Charlotte by the waist and moved her over so she'd be to the side of the door and not in the line of sight by whoever answered. Hall softly knocked a couple times and waited for it to open.

Only a few seconds after knocking, the door quickly opened. Benny opened the door, and though he instantly recognized Hall, with his arm in a sling, there was nothing he could do against the dangerous man. Before he was able to scream out to warn the others, Hall delivered a knockout kind of punch on the man's face, sending him stumbling backwards until his back hit a desk. Hall rushed into the room and looked to his right, seeing the man with glasses sitting there. Ricky started to get up, anticipating a fight, but Hall gave him a thrust kick to the ribs, sending him flying over the chair, which landed on top of him. Kowalski was sitting behind his desk and was stunned with what was happening. He reached for a desk drawer and opened it, but wasn't able to get to his gun in time, as Hall already had the gun Charlotte gave him pointed right at his head.

"I wouldn't do it," Hall said, almost goading him to try.

For some reason, Kowalski broke out a huge grin. He was sort of impressed at the man's gumption. He would have never thought the man would have come there, broken into his office, and held a gun on him. He slowly put his hands in the air, though only midway between his waist and his head.

"You want me to close that," Kowalski said, looking down at the drawer.

"You better do it slowly."

Kowalski lowered his left hand cautiously, making sure Hall didn't think he was reaching for his gun. Though he didn't believe Hall was there to kill him, if he was, he would have done it already, Kowalski wasn't ready to test that belief by making a dumb move. He knew there was no way he'd get to the gun before Hall blew a hole through him. His only move at this point was to play along with whatever Hall wanted. After closing the drawer, Kowalski looked behind him at his chair.

"Mind if I sit?"

"Not there," Hall said. He looked at one of the chairs along the wall and waved his gun at Kowalski to choose one of those seats. Hall didn't want him sitting behind his desk, just in case he had some secret button to push or some stashed gun that he could break out.

Kowalski complied with the man's wishes, walking over to one of the other chairs. As he sat down, Ricky pushed the chair off of him and got to his feet. Hall pointed at the chair to him as well, wanting him to sit down. Charlotte had long since closed the door at that point and was just watching the proceedings. Benny had gotten to his knees, but just stayed there, waiting for his orders. He was in no condition to challenge anyone.

"You, sit on the floor over there," Hall said, directing Benny to the wall. "Sit with your back against the wall."

As Benny moved, Charlotte hurried past him, taking Kowalski's chair behind the desk.

"If any of you move, I'll kill you on the spot," Hall said.

"I don't think you got the guts," Kowalski replied. "I don't think you could kill anybody. If you could, you probably would have by now."

"I was in the military. I've killed lots of people. I know how. Don't mistake me allowing you to live as a weakness in thinking that I can't. You keep pressing, you'll find out how wrong you are."

Kowalski wasn't sure he believed any of that, but it certainly gave him something to think about.

"So what do you want?" Kowalski asked. "Why are you here gracing us with your presence?"

"I want you to stop chasing us. Don't come after us anymore."

"And if we don't?"

"Then you won't like what happens to you," Hall answered. "Next time I see you I'm coming up shooting."

"Maybe we might do the same."

"Or we can just stop all that nonsense if you stop looking for us. You're gonna stop looking for both of us. You're gonna stop talking to her family. You're just gonna stop period."

Kowalski briefly looked at Charlotte, knowing she'd talked to her father. He then turned his attention back to Hall. "Or you can just give us back what you've taken and we can forget all this. Give me my merchandise back and I can forget this incident ever happened and you can both get on with your lives without fear of me coming."

Hall started to get agitated. "How many times do I have to tell you I don't know what you're talking about? I don't have your stupid merchandise."

Kowalski rolled his head back and looked at the ceiling. Hall could tell he didn't believe him.

"Do you really think I'd come here and do this if I still had your stuff? I don't know if your stuff is drugs, money, gold coins, or someone's stolen stamp collection. If I had it, don't you think I'd be long gone by now instead of coming here and telling you I don't have it?"

Ricky looked at his boss, seeds of doubt entering his mind. "Maybe he's right, boss."

"Shut up," Kowalski replied. "You don't get paid to think."

"Maybe you should try listening to him," Hall said.

"I was specifically told to meet Brandon Hall on the way back from San Diego. He was the one who had my merchandise. Now we checked the passenger list... we even checked it twice, there was no other Brandon Hall traveling that day. No other Hall. No other anything that even closely resembled your name."

"Whoever told you that was wrong."

"Why would someone give me your name if you weren't the one carrying my stuff?"

Hall shrugged. "Maybe that person was trying to divert your attention to me while the real person was getting away."

Kowalski was starting to get nervous that maybe the man really was telling the truth. He wiped a patch of sweat off his forehead, thinking about whether they really were set up. Both Ricky and Benny looked at their boss. They were more inclined to believe Hall's story than not. Kowalski looked at each of his underlings and could tell by their faces that they thought

Hall was leveling with them. The longer he thought about it, the more he had doubts. He did think it was strange that Hall would go there and try to convince him he was innocent if he really wasn't. It wouldn't have been the smart play.

"Let's just say I believe this story of yours," Kowalski said. "And I'm not saying that I do. But if it's true, why would someone give me your name if you're not involved?"

"I already told you. Whoever told you it was me, actually gave it to someone else. That way while you're chasing me, they're cutting you out of the deal. Is the person who told you it was me capable of doing that?"

Kowalski looked at both of his henchmen, not believing that Palumbo would have set them up like that. They'd always had a good relationship previous to that. Never had any arguments or bad deals. But a million dollar deal had a way of changing relationships, whether they were good or not. A million dollars all for himself was better than Palumbo splitting it in half with his partners. Ricky nudged his boss on the arm with his elbow.

"I'm thinking, I'm thinking," Kowalski belligerently replied.

"Listen, if I had your stuff, even if I had it by accident, I'd give it to you by now," Hall said. "Just to make all this stuff go away. But I don't and I never did."

"So how did your name come up? Someone just pick it out of the air?"

Hall shrugged. "I have no idea. Couldn't even venture a guess. Maybe they closed their eyes and picked someone. Maybe they looked at my picture and thought I fit the part. I don't really know. All I know is you're looking for the wrong man."

Much to his chagrin, the longer Hall spoke, the more Kowalski was inclined to believe him. He'd been around long enough to know that if Hall was really guilty, it was unlikely he'd be there right now. He'd still be running.

"OK. Say I do believe you," Kowalski said. "A lot's gone down in the past twenty-four hours."

"All I want is my name cleared with you guys," Hall replied.

Charlotte looked at him like he forgot something. "And me too?"

"Oh. Yeah. Her too."

"What was all that business back at the apartment with you two?" Kowalski asked.

"I went up to the third floor and was waiting for you guys," Hall answered. "I saw Charlotte come out of her apartment and I worried about her getting mixed up in everything. I didn't want to get hurt, so I went over to her and pushed her back into her apartment. Then you know the rest."

Kowalski sighed, looking angrier by the second, feeling like he'd been led astray. He now realized they'd made a terrible mistake. He was fuming that Palumbo had backstabbed him. And he knew it was

Palumbo behind it. He knew Palumbo picked some patsy on a train, hoping that Kowalski and his crew would spend so much time, perhaps as much as a few weeks trying to track down what really happened. By that time, Palumbo would have successfully gotten rid of everything and pocketed the money all by himself.

"It's Palumbo!" Ricky said, finally saying the man's name.

"He's made a fool out of us," Benny said.

Kowalski hushed the both of them, still not wanting to invoke Palumbo's name publicly, though he didn't know that Hall was already aware of the situation. "Shut up, the both of you."

"So what's it gonna be?" Hall asked.

Kowalski looked at both of his men. "You know, based on the situation I'm in, I'm not really in much of a position to argue. I could say anything right now just to get you out of here, then do whatever I want after that."

Hall stared at him for a moment, then made a calculated gamble. He lowered his gun, letting it hang down by his side. With the three men not armed, he didn't feel he had much to fear from them. Even if they tried to rush him, one of them had a broken arm, and the other looked like his nose was broken by the size of it and the bandage that was draped across it.

"I'm not here to play games," Hall said. "If I had the stuff, I'd be long gone."

Kowalski, still a serious look on his face, rose out of

his chair. He took a few steps toward Hall, not stopping until they were only a few inches away from each other. Though Hall didn't believe that Kowalski was going to throw the first punch, he was ready for anything. Charlotte, fearing more fisticuffs was about to go down, backed away to make sure she was not in hitting range. The two men just stood there for a minute, staring at each other, neither backing down.

"OK," Kowalski finally said. "We're good. For now. But if I change my mind later, or I think you're giving me some snow job here to throw me further off the track, I'll be back."

"I'm not going anywhere. As a matter of fact, someone threw me under the bus and tried to make a sucker out of me. I'm not just gonna let that go either. I'm gonna find who's responsible for it."

Kowalski snickered, though he could appreciate the intent behind his threat. "Listen, if I'm right about what's going on here, you're gonna have a long line ahead of you, and I promise you that we'll probably get there first. But I'll tell you what I do, if I do find out, I'll send you a postcard to let you know."

With both sides feeling like they had an understanding between each other, the tension in the room slowly dissipated. Kowalski started walking around freely, moving past Hall and around his desk. As he sat down in his chair again, Charlotte scurried around to move next to Hall again.

"Is there anything else?" Kowalski asked.

"Nope. That's it," Hall replied.

"Well then I guess our business here is finished."

"Yeah. I guess it is."

"We chased you around a bit, you broke some bones, we'll call it even."

Satisfied that their business was done and there was nothing left to discuss, Hall and Charlotte backed away to leave the room. They took Kowalski at his word that he believed them, but they weren't ready to turn their backs to him just yet. Once they left the office, they walked down the hallway and saw the guard that Hall previously had taken out. The man was holding his arm, but as he saw Hall approaching, braced himself for another fight. Hall put his arms up to let him know he wasn't looking for trouble. He patted the man on his good arm as they walked past.

"Sorry about that," Hall said.

Hall and Charlotte kept walking, continually looking over their shoulder to make sure no one was coming. No one was though. They immediately left the club and headed for their car. Once inside, they both breathed a little sigh of relief.

"That went much better than I expected it to," Charlotte said.

"Yeah, you and me both."

11

Not long after Hall left the nightclub, Kowalski put in a call to Palumbo to have a meeting. He wanted to clear the air and get the truth out of what was likely to be his former partner. Kowalski didn't say what he wanted, that way Palumbo didn't have time to prepare for their discussion and think of some lie beforehand. They agreed to meet at Kowalski's night-club at ten the next morning. Palumbo tried to avoid doing business at night. Whether it was actually true or not, it was his opinion that when deals went bad, they happened after dark. People seemed to always be on better behavior during the day.

When Palumbo arrived for his meeting, he was accompanied by three well-built bodyguards who accompanied him wherever he went. A man of his position and stature was bound to run into trouble now and then, plus it helped to flex a little extra muscle when it was needed. Especially after an assassination attempt was made on his life about ten years ago by an overanxious underling who thought it was his time to rise to power. Now, he didn't go anywhere without being heavily protected.

After being led into Kowalski's office, he immediately knew something was up when he saw his partner's four henchmen standing there. He never felt the need to have them all there before for one of their meetings. Kowalski usually had one, maybe two men with him, which was usually expected. But to have four in there was a message to Palumbo. At least that's how he took it. It was a show of force and aggression.

Before taking a seat, Palumbo stood near the door, his three guards behind him. He sized the situation up before doing or saying anything. He'd seen them all in better, healthier days. Though Kowalski had made him aware of the problems he was having securing his merchandise, he didn't tell him the lengths of the problem he'd been having. Hall certainly had done a number on all of them.

"Have a seat," Kowalski said, extending his arm to the chair in front of the desk.

Palumbo obliged, a smirk on his face as he glanced at Kowalski's muscle. He wasn't intimidated in the least at the attempt by his partner to show some force. He was a very confident man, probably overly so quite often, bordering on cocky at times. He was a powerful man that didn't believe he could be touched. Not by the law, not by his partners-in-crime, not anyone. He looked the part of a flashy and wealthy man, wearing thousand dollar suits, expensive watches and jewelry. He was in his late thirties, and though he was just an average-looking man, had a great gift in being able to read people and situations. He knew what made people tick, what they desired, what they wanted, and what they were willing to do to get it. He was a great judge of character. He was also a master manipulator. He could get anyone, friend or foe, to believe almost anything he was saying. He had a gift of spinning anything he wanted to make it sound like whoever he was talking to was getting a great deal or it was the best thing that ever happened to them, usually while he was benefiting the most.

While Palumbo initially began his criminal career as a low level trickster committing fraud for various employers, he didn't like sharing or parting with a good portion of the money. It wasn't long before he started his own organization, building it from the ground up. He started as a small-time operator, but quickly built his business into the multi-million dollar operation it was today. He was involved in just about anything that made him money. As far as he was concerned, nothing was off limits. If there was major money to be made, he wanted to be in on it.

The clean-shaven Palumbo ran his hand over his slicked back black hair, pretending he wasn't bothered by what he was seeing. He reached into his shirt pocket and took out an expensive cigar, lighting it with a smile on his face.

"Nothing like a good cigar in the morning," Palumbo said, looking at it lovingly. "Quality stuff those Cubans put out. Real quality stuff."

"Yeah, great," Rex said, not giving a crap, finally sitting down himself.

Palumbo puffed his cigar and sent some smoke into the air. "So what is all this about, Rex? It sounded like it was urgent."

"It is."

"So what's the problem?" In reality, unless it somehow concerned his welfare, Palumbo wasn't particularly interested in whatever the issue was. He had mostly come out of courtesy to a business partner. "And what's happened to the boys?" he asked with a hint of a laugh, somewhat amused by their rough-looking appearance.

"Brandon Hall's what happened to them."

"Oh, yes, yes, what's going on with that?" Palumbo asked, though he didn't sound very concerned. Not as concerned as one would expect over a million dollar deal. "Have you found him again yet over your clumsy operation on the train?"

"You might say that."

"So what's happened? What's being done?"

"You for starters," Rex answered.

"And what's that supposed to mean?"

"Well for one..."

Palumbo interrupted his host, hoping he wasn't going to get into specific details about anything. He had a rule that he didn't discuss any business deals in front of others. Only the people he was directly doing business with and the guards that he trusted. Anyone else was a liability and potential leak as far as he was concerned.

"I hope you're not going to say something in regards to a specific deal, Rex," Palumbo said, waving his finger in the air. "You know my rule on that."

"Well I am."

Palumbo leaned back, a disappointed look on his face before puffing on his cigar again to calm him down. "Tell them to leave the room first," he said, pointing his thumb at Rex's men as he blew more smoke into the air.

Rex held his ground though, not willing to give in to a man he thought was cheating him. "Only if yours do too."

Palumbo took another puff of his cigar as he stared at Kowalski, thinking of his proposition. Mostly out of curiosity about what was about to be said, Palumbo turned his head to the left and threw his left hand in the air, waving his fingers at his guards to let them know it was OK to leave the room. Seeing that he was agreeable to it, Kowalski nodded at his men to do the same. Both sets of guards then left the room, leaving only the two leaders there alone to discuss business. Both teams of guards stood in the hallway, just outside the door, staring each other down. Neither would say a word to each other for the entire time they were there.

"So what is this about?" Palumbo said, puffing on his cigar, not seeming to have a care in the world. "Why do you look so angry?"

"I think you know what this is about. And I always look angry when I've had a million dollars snatched out from under me."

"A most unfortunate situation to be sure. I cannot believe it has gotten to this point."

"Me neither."

"What I don't understand is why, when this man is probably close to leaving the state by now, why you and your men are here doing nothing?"

"He hasn't left the state," Kowalski replied. "I know where he is."

"Oh? Then where is our merchandise?"

"It's a little more complicated than that."

"Such as?"

"Such as he doesn't have it. At least I don't think he does."

"Then who does? He passed it on to another party?"

"Why don't you and I stop playing games here and come clean with each other?"

With the cigar in his mouth, Palumbo threw both of his hands up in the air to each side of him. "Isn't that what we've always done?"

Kowalski got out of his chair and started pacing

around, his calmness slowly evaporating into a seething anger as he continuously thought about getting cheated. "Late last night I was paid a visit from Mr. Hall."

Palumbo's eyes almost bulged out of its sockets, surprised at the news. "You mean he came here? At the club? To see you?"

"Yeah. Imagine that."

"I don't understand. The man who stole from us, who has slipped through your fingers, has gift wrapped himself to you by coming here... and you say you still do not have our merchandise? What is going on?"

Kowalski stopped pacing and angrily looked at his guest. He forcefully leaned on his knuckles as he pounded them onto the desk. "You're what's going on. You think I'm a fool?"

"Of course not, Rex. Get a hold of yourself."

"I know what you've done. I know what you're doing. And I'm not gonna sit still for it."

"Rex, my friend..."

"Don't friend me. You're two-timing me. You little arrogant piss-ant. You no good piece of..."

Palumbo put his finger in the air to stop Kowalski from saying something he would regret. He didn't let anyone talk to him or curse him out like that. "Careful of what you say, my friend. I would watch your tone before you say something you cannot take back."

"I am watching my tone. And I ain't your friend. But anyway, about this Hall guy, the entire time I've been on him, he's proclaimed his innocence. On the train, at his apartment, and when he visited me last night."

"Everyone professes to be innocent. You know that."

"I know. That's why I didn't believe him at first."

"So why now?"

"Like you said… he could've been anywhere by now. I didn't know where the hell he was. But you know what I do know?"

"What might that be?"

"I know that guilty men don't waltz into a man's office that he just stole from still saying he didn't do it, when he could've been hundreds of miles away. That just doesn't seem logical does it?"

"Life is full of many things, men included, that don't make much sense."

"That may well be. But I think something else is going on here," Kowalski said.

"Which is?"

"I think that package never left its destination."

"What are you saying? Someone else took it?"

"I'm saying that you set this whole thing up so you could pocket the money all by yourself."

"Rex, would I do such a thing?" Palumbo asked with a smile on his face, not concerned by the allegation. "All for a few measly million dollars?"

"Yeah, I think you would do that. And I think you did do that."

"I would urge you to reconsider what you're saying and think of the repercussions of such."

"I've already thought of them and I'm not taking back any of it," Kowalski replied. "I set this deal up for you. I brought it to you because you had connections that I didn't have."

"And you were being rewarded handsomely for it."

"Were is the key word. You decided to bypass my end of it."

"I'm honestly not sure what I can do to convince you this isn't true."

"You can't. You got the list of passengers on the train, picked out Hall's name for some reason, maybe because you knew he could fight back against us, that way we'd be chasing our tails for a while. And while we were doing that, nobody would be looking at you with an extra million dollars in your pocket. That package was never aboard the train, was it?"

Palumbo laughed. "I don't know what you wish me to say."

"That you did it would suffice for starters."

"Rex, you come to me with this outlandish plot, accusing me of some monstrous behavior, and I have yet to hear anything but wild accusations. I presume you have some evidence to show me? Something to show that I have actually done what you say I have?"

There was silence between the two as they stared at

each other. Palumbo was trying to put the pressure on and intimidate his opponent into backing down. Kowalski already knew their relationship had been severed and was past the point of no return. He wasn't backing down. Though he didn't have evidence, he knew it was true.

Palumbo was the one who told him that Hall would be carrying the bag. If Hall was innocent, as Kowalski now believed he was, then that only pointed to one man. The man that set him up. And Kowalski wasn't going to let him off the hook, no matter what the repercussions were after this. He was prepared for a war if that's what resulted from it.

For his part, Palumbo was growing tired of the conversation. His charade was obviously discovered, but he wasn't about to admit any complicity in the scheme. Whichever way Kowalski wanted to play it from now on was fine with him. If he wanted to forget the entire ordeal, Palumbo just might do that. If he wanted a fight, Palumbo was just as willing to oblige.

"So in taking that we seem to be at a standstill, how do you expect for us to move past this?" Palumbo asked.

"I don't expect nothing. I want my half. And you're gonna give it to me."

"And if I don't?" Palumbo asked, coming the closest he had yet to actually admitting it.

"Then you better start looking over your shoulder from now on."

Palumbo grinned, taking another puff of his cigar. "I believe we have nothing left to discuss."

Kowalski pointed at Palumbo before his guest got up. "Listen, you, you give me my half of the deal and I might forget this thing ever happened. I mean, you and me will never do business again, but at least I won't threaten to kill you. But if you keep on playing hard-ball with me, I promise you that you'll live to regret it."

Palumbo smiled again, not appearing to take the threat with much urgency. He finally did get up, but didn't leave yet without giving Kowalski another stare down. The two locked eyes for another minute, both having bad intentions in their mind. Each of them figured their next meeting would not be as peaceful as this one.

"I believe that we have an understanding," Palumbo said.

"Wait a minute. You said it yourself. Are you really gonna ruin what we got going on for a measly million dollars?"

An evil smile crept across Palumbo's face. "Like I said, Rex. We understand each other."

Kowalski nodded, knowing that was as close to an admittance of guilt as he was going to get. "Indeed we do. Hope those guards of yours are as good at shooting as they are at looking tough."

"Oh, they are. I would be careful of what you wish for, Rex. I would let this go if I was you."

"Well you ain't me."

"Thank goodness for that. By the looks of you and your men, you have a hard enough time handling one man. I'd like to know how you plan on handling me and mine."

"Don't worry. I've got something in mind."

"I'm sure you do."

"This can all be avoided if you just give me what's mine," Kowalski said.

"Don't worry, Rex. You'll get what's coming to you. I promise you that."

Palumbo took another puff of his cigar, blowing the smoke directly into his former friend's face. Kowalski watched his ex-business partner leave the room, just as cocky and confident as ever, and figured that would be his undoing. As tough as Kowalski was, he knew every man could be beaten under the right circumstances. Palumbo was no different. The fact that he didn't think anyone could best him would be what came back to bite him. As soon as the door closed behind Palumbo, Kowalski gritted his teeth and pounded his right hand onto the top of his desk.

Kowalski's men waited in the hallway until Palumbo and his goons had gone, making sure they didn't come back and give them an unhealthy surprise. One of the men followed them through the club to make sure they left. The others went back into Kowalski's office, anxious to hear how the meeting went.

"What happened, Rex?" Ricky asked.

"Yeah, what'd he say?" Benny asked. "Did he admit to anything?"

"Not in so many words," Kowalski replied. "But he did it. Just like Hall said."

"Palumbo didn't look so happy when he left," Ricky said.

"He shouldn't. Because pretty soon he's gonna be a dead man."

"Rex, you know what you're saying?"

"I know exactly what I'm saying. Nobody cheats me out of a million dollars and gets away with it. Not Palumbo, not anybody. I don't care how big and tough he thinks he and his organization is."

Ricky and Benny warily looked at each other, knowing what that meant. They'd be continuously looking over their shoulders from now on.

"Are you sure there's not another way?" Benny asked, not liking the idea of getting shot at.

"There isn't one," Kowalski replied. "I gave him a chance to make good on it but he refused. This is the way he wants it. So this is the way he's gonna get it."

12

They drove around for about an hour before finally settling on a hotel. They passed a couple of smaller ones that looked like they'd seen better days, but Hall didn't want to make Charlotte spend the night in some insect-infested place that was about to fall down. Not that he was looking for a five-star hotel either, just something where they weren't awake all night batting flies away and was pleasant enough for a good sleep.

After finding what would be considered a three-star hotel in a nice area, they finally checked in and went up to their room on the fourth floor. Luckily they got one with double beds, so Hall didn't have to sleep on the floor. Not that Charlotte would have made him, as she probably would have offered him to sleep in the same one as hers. But now they didn't have that problem as the two of them sat down on the interior edge of their respective beds, facing each other.

Hall laughed. "There was a small time today when I wasn't sure we'd actually ever get to this point."

"What point?"

"Bed."

Charlotte laughed as well. "Yeah. I guess I had the same thought."

"I just wanna say I'm sorry again for everything."

Charlotte just smiled and shook her head while giving a semblance of a shrug, not knowing what else to do. "It's OK. It's not your fault."

"Yeah, well, maybe not, but I'm still the reason you're here."

"Yeah, and if you hadn't done it, then maybe I would've gotten caught up in it, anyway. Maybe all this would have happened, anyway."

"You really do believe I'm innocent of everything, right?"

"Of course."

"You say that now, but there was a time when you had your doubts, didn't you?"

Charlotte grinned, thinking back to when he first barged into her apartment. She really did think he might have been crazy. "Maybe a little bit," she said, putting her thumb and index fingers close together, only a tiny bit of space between them. "So what's the plan now?"

"Sleep."

"I mean after that. Kowalski seemed to believe you."

"Yeah, that's a good first step," Hall said. "I don't think we need to worry about them anymore."

"Then what are we doing here? Why don't we just go home?"

"What if his boss convinces him otherwise?"

"Oh. Yeah," Charlotte said, a dejected look on her face.

Hall reached over and grabbed hold of her hand, rubbing it. "Hey, it'll only be another day or two. I promise."

"Sure about that?"

"Yes."

"But if Kowalski does believe you, like he seemed to, wouldn't that mean the problem is now between him and Palumbo?"

"Well, yeah, but what if Palumbo wins?" Hall asked. "He used me once. If he thinks he got away with it, he can do it again, and keep using my name as long as he thinks he can. What if next week or next week he does the same thing with someone else? What if in a couple months the same thing happens to me?"

Charlotte nodded, understanding his point, even if all she wanted to do was go home and sleep in her own bed. She could understand his reservations. She let out a deep sigh before going into the bathroom to get ready for bed. As she walked into the bathroom, Hall stared at the back of her long blonde hair swaying off her shoulders. He just thought of how great she was. He couldn't imagine a lot of people, men or women, who would have acted the way she did after getting thrown into this situation. She really made the best of it without complaining about what it was doing to her life.

Once the door closed behind her, and Hall's eyes were no longer on her, he knew he had to end this soon. He couldn't let her be mixed up in this thing for days, or god forbid, weeks or months. He had to find a way to end it. And that would mean going up the food chain, moving on from Kowalski to the man that set it up. Palumbo.

Hall's thoughts on Palumbo were interrupted when he heard the bathroom door open. He looked over at Charlotte coming out, a part of him thinking of movies he'd seen where the woman goes into the bathroom fully clothed and came out wearing some sexy type of lingerie or nothing at all even. This was not one of those movie moments. He watched her come back to her bed, still wearing the same clothes as she'd been wearing all day. With his eyes still fixated on her body as she sat down, she could tell he was thinking about something.

"What is it?" Charlotte asked, afraid she looked funny or something.

Her soft voice woke up from his trance. "Hmm? Oh, nothing. Nothing."

"Then why were you looking at me like that? Do I have something on me?"

"No, nothing. Honest."

"Is there something you're not telling me?" she asked, turning her head and lifting her arm to take a sniff.

Hall laughed, "no, it's nothing like that. You're fine."

Charlotte barely lifted her butt off the bed and playfully shoved him on the shoulder so he'd open up to her. "No, what?" she said with a laugh. "It's obviously something, just tell me."

Hall put his hand over his mouth and shook his head. He was too embarrassed to say. Charlotte was not taking that for an answer and grabbed his wrist and pulled it down off his face.

"No, I am not letting you go to bed until you tell me why you were looking at me like that."

Hall turned away, with a goofy-looking grin on his face before finally relenting. "OK, I'll tell you."

Charlotte sat back down on the bed as she worried about what was going to come out of his mouth.

"OK, I was just picturing one of those movie scenes, where the girl goes into the bathroom fully clothed and comes back out in something revealing."

After saying it, Hall put his hand over his face and eyes, almost afraid to look at her after saying such a thing. Charlotte balled her hand into a fist, putting it over her mouth as she looked down, also a little embarrassed at first. With her head still down, she peered up at him, Hall still looking away. Though it was a little embarrassing at first, she thought it was nice how he thought that way of her. Even if it wasn't how he meant it, it'd been a long time since she saw a man looking or thinking of her like that. It was kind of nice. Seeing as how Hall still seemed embarrassed, she tried to make him feel a little more comfortable.

"Sorry I don't have an extra set of clothes to change into for you," Charlotte said with a chuckle.

"No, it's not that," Hall said, waving his hand around as he finally looked at her again. "I don't know why I had thought of it. It was stupid. Sorry."

"I didn't think it was stupid."

Hall looked at her and couldn't take his eyes off her pretty face. He had a strong urge to lean across and plant a kiss on her lips, but he thought it'd be an inappropriate gesture considering the fix they were in. Especially with the jam they were in, and sleeping together in a hotel room, it could be a pretty uncomfortable night if she wasn't receptive to it. So Hall fought his impulses and tore his eyes off her, thinking of something to change the subject.

"So I guess tomorrow we have to find Palumbo," Hall said, clearing his throat.

"Why? He's not going to clear you."

"I'm gonna make him clear me. Either that or we have to find that bag."

"He's probably already got it by now," Charlotte said.

"Maybe not. What if someone else on the train had it?"

Charlotte shrugged, still not seeing the point. "So? Wouldn't he still have given it to Palumbo by now?"

"Maybe. It's only been a day though. I guess it depends on what was in the bag and where it was going after that. Was it going to Palumbo? Or was Kowalski giving the bag to another third party in exchange for money?"

"What difference does it make?"

"Because the way Kowalski was talking about it, he said the stuff in that bag was worth a million dollars to him. So it wasn't money in the bag."

"OK?"

"So if it was something else, it'd have to be sold for the money," Hall explained. "That means it'd have to be traded to someone else for that cash, right?"

"Yeah."

"So that means Palumbo probably doesn't have it. Somebody else had the bag and is making the exchange instead of Kowalski."

"I still don't get it," Charlotte said. "Why go through all this nonsense just to tick Kowalski off? Why not just let him do the deal?"

Hall threw his hands up, not having a clear picture

of it yet either. "Only thing I can think of is that he wanted Kowalski out of the way somehow. Or maybe Palumbo would get a bigger slice of the money without Kowalski. If Kowalski's share of the deal was a million dollars, maybe Palumbo had second thoughts about giving away that much money?"

"Yeah, could be."

With the time fast approaching midnight, the two of them figured they should get to bed, knowing they likely had another long day ahead of them tomorrow. Before lying down, Charlotte took the opportunity to kid him one last time for the day.

"Should I go back to the bathroom again for you?"

Hall couldn't help but laugh, despite being made fun of. "Don't start," he said, lying down.

"OK. But I do have one small request for the morning."

"What's that?"

"I need to get a change of clothes. I know some guys are more than happy to stay in the same clothes for two, three, four days, even a week. But I am not. I need new clothes every day. Do you think we can stop at my apartment in the morning so I can change?"

Hall looked at her, the expression on his face telling her all she needed to know. It was a no. "I'm still not sure that's a good idea."

"Why not? Kowalski's not going to be there."

"What if Palumbo convinced him that I'm lying? Or what if Palumbo's watching the place himself?"

Charlotte grunted, not liking the thought of being in the same clothes for another day. It just felt icky to her. But she also knew her partner wasn't likely to change his mind. "Fine."

"If it makes you feel any better, we can just stop at a department store real quick after breakfast."

"I guess that'll work."

"Somehow I thought it would."

"What's that supposed to mean?" Charlotte asked. "You better not be giving me that stereotype about women and shopping. You know, oh, I just love to shop until my feet fall off and all that?"

Hall put his hands up, not wanting to get into an argument, seeing that she was a little sensitive about the subject. "All I said was..."

"You thought because I'm a woman I would just love the chance to shop? Like I'd be salivating or something?"

Hall just looked up to the ceiling and shook his head. "I said nothing of the kind."

"Good, because just because I'm a woman, doesn't mean I love to shop."

"I will certainly remember that."

"Good, because I really don't like shopping all that much."

"I am beyond delighted to know that."

"Just so you remember."

"Believe me, I promise you I will not forget."

"Good. Well, good night," Charlotte said, turning

off the light over her bed and rolling onto her side, which was her favorite sleeping position.

"Night."

"Hopefully tomorrow's a better day."

"I certainly hope so."

13

Hall woke up and yawned as he sat up. As he rubbed his eyes, he glanced at Charlotte's bed and saw that she wasn't in it. He turned his head around in every direction, then got up. Considering the bathroom door was already open, he figured she wasn't in there, but he took a peak, anyway. He headed into the kitchen, not finding a trace of her anywhere. He was about to grab his phone when he heard what sounded like the key card being put in the door. Hall rushed over to stand behind the door before it opened. Once it did, he was relieved to see it was Charlotte coming in. It's who he expected it to be, but he wasn't about to take chances these days.

Charlotte turned around to close the door and let out a high-pitched scream when he saw his outline standing there. She almost dropped the bag she had in her arms. She put her hand on her chest and closed her eyes, taking a deep breath.

"Why would you do that to me?!"

"What?" Hall replied.

"Scare me like that."

"I wasn't trying to."

"You always just stand behind doors when people walk in?"

"Well in my defense, I didn't know where you were, or who was coming in."

"Uh, yes, you did."

"Did what?" Hall asked.

"Know where I was going."

"I did not. How would I know where you were going? I just woke up, and you weren't here."

"Because before I left, I told you."

Hall rolled his eyes and shook his head, positive that she did not. "No you didn't."

"I woke up and at seven o'clock and you were still sleeping. Instead of waiting around for you to get up, I figured I'd go out and get breakfast. You were still sleeping, so I tapped you on the shoulder and told you that I was going out to get something."

"I don't remember that."

"Well you opened your eyes, barely looked at me, then mumbled something completely unintelligent, and then buried your head back in your pillow. So I just left."

"Oh," Hall said. "What time is it, anyway?"

"About eight o'clock."

"What'd you get?" Hall said, looking at the bag.

Charlotte went over to the counter and put it down, taking items out of it. "I wasn't sure what you liked or wanted so I just got a few things. Couple donuts, bagels, and muffins."

Hall went over and inspected them. "I'll take a bagel. And a muffin."

"Here's some orange juice too," Charlotte said, handing him a small bottle.

"Thank you."

The two sat there eating next to each other, neither saying a word. After a few minutes, Hall finally broke the silence.

"Sleep all right?"

"Eh, it was OK I guess," Charlotte answered. "Woke up a few times and..."

"And what?"

"Nothing really. Just thinking about everything I guess."

"I'm sorry."

"For what?"

"Just you being here."

Charlotte sighed, getting tired of listening to him beat himself up over getting her involved. "Would you please stop saying that?"

"I'm sorry. I just can't help but think..."

"There's nothing you could have done. It was just dumb luck that I stepped out of the apartment when I did. Sometimes that's just the way it goes. If you did nothing and let me keep on walking, maybe one of those guys hurts or kills me on their way to you."

"Yeah."

"But you gotta stop getting on yourself about this," Charlotte said. "It's not going to get you anywhere. Whatever's happened is done and we can't change it now. Now we just gotta deal with it and move on. And you need to move on."

Hall looked at her and smiled, letting out the faintest part of a laugh.

"What?"

"Nothing."

"Why are you laughing at me?" Charlotte asked.

"I'm not really. I was just thinking how special you are."

Charlotte's face started getting red and she looked away. "I'm not really."

"Yes you are. There's not many people who would have the same attitude as you do about all this."

"I just choose not to dwell on the past, that's all. Doesn't make me special."

"Well in any case, I'll still always probably feel like I owe you something."

"I'll tell you what, when this is finally over, if you still feel like you owe me something, you can take me to dinner."

Hall smiled, thinking that was an offer he couldn't refuse. "Sounds like a date or something."

Charlotte shrugged, thinking she may have misread the signs. "You don't have to if you'd rather not."

"No, it's not that, I'd like to. I really would. Just seems like you're letting me off cheaply."

"You might not feel that way after the dinner's done. I'm not talking about some cheap fast food place. I mean like a real fancy dinner. And it's on you."

"That'll be money well worth paying."

Once they were finished eating, they started getting ready to start the day.

"You need me to go in the bathroom again for you," Charlotte kidded.

Hall's shoulder slumped, and he couldn't help but laugh. "Not again. You're really never gonna let me live that down, are you?"

A devilish smile came over her face. "Yeah, I really kind of doubt it."

"Don't forget, we need to go shopping first. You know, because I love it so."

Hall moved his mouth around, biting his tongue, knowing that she was likely to twist around anything he said. She certainly had some spunk to him, he thought. But he liked it. He didn't mind a woman who could give it back to him. And she could certainly give it as much as she got it.

"This isn't going to take long, is it?"

"Shouldn't," Charlotte replied. "I'm only going to

get a few things. Another shirt or two, another pair of pants, socks, under... well, that's basically it."

"So half the day?" Hall said, not actually believing it would take that long, but wanting to rib her a little.

"No, I'm not someone who spends all day looking for one thing. As soon as I find something, that's it, I don't keep looking for something better. OK, Mr. Smartypants?"

"Yeah, I guess."

With not having to pack, they were able to check out of the hotel pretty quickly. There was a department store only a couple blocks away from the hotel, so their pit stop wouldn't take too long. When they got there, Charlotte went into the store by herself, so Hall used the time alone to think about the rest of their day. Plus, he didn't feel all that comfortable standing inside while Charlotte looked for clothes.

Hall racked his brain trying to think of the best play from here. All he could think about was seeing Palumbo and knocking his head into the wall a few dozen times, but he knew that wasn't the best option. He thought of breaking into Palumbo's house, but he assumed he wouldn't just have damaging evidence against him just lying around in plain sight. It seemed too chancy and was a risk that didn't seem like it had a high degree of probability in paying off. They needed to find the guy who actually did have the bag. How to do that was the next question. They would have to hack into the train system to see the passenger list, but he didn't have the skills to do that. He was pretty sure that Charlotte didn't either, even though she seemed to be better at computer work than he was.

Hall was so deep in thought that he didn't even see Charlotte coming. With two bags in hand, she was already wearing new clothes, changing in the bathroom after she paid for it. Hall was slightly startled and jumped when he heard the passenger door open and saw the outline of someone coming in. After calming down, he looked at the new clothes Charlotte was wearing. Then he looked at the time.

"Wow. Half an hour."

"That's not that long," Charlotte protested.

"No, I mean, it feels like you just went in there. Went by quick."

"Oh. I noticed you seemed to be in another world."

"Yeah, just thinking about what to do from here."

"And did you come up with anything?"

"I think we need to find the guy that really did have the bag," Hall replied.

"Why? What good would that do?"

"Leverage. If we get the bag and hold it hostage, I can get myself out of this."

"Wouldn't it make more sense to just go to Palumbo directly?"

"I think there are a couple problems with that."

"Such as?"

"Well, if I go to Palumbo now, what am I gonna do? Only thing I can do is kill him."

"You can uncover evidence that he framed you."

"How am I gonna do that?" Hall asked. "You think he's just gonna leave an email or print out a text message and leave it on his desk for me to find?"

"Good point."

"Plus he's probably got a ton of guards around him so it's not gonna be that easy to get to him."

"So you think it's gonna be easier finding some mysterious guy on a train with a bag that you don't even know was really there?"

Hall made a face as he scratched his ear, knowing they had a tall task in front of them. He then put his hand on his forehead, obviously frustrated. "I don't know what to do."

Charlotte put her hand on his knee, feeling bad for him. "We'll think of something."

"I can't just call the police and ask them, they're not gonna tell me anything."

"Not likely."

"You don't happen to be able to hack into the train system and get the passenger list, can you?"

"Excuse me? You want me to commit a crime?"

"Well don't look at it as committing a crime," Hall answered. "Think of it as helping a friend with an extremely time sensitive problem."

"Uh, no. No."

"Why can't you? I thought you wanted this over with."

"I do."

"So why won't you do it?"

"Because I don't know how," Charlotte plainly answered.

"Oh. Well why didn't you just come out and say that?"

"I don't know."

"I thought you were good with computers?"

"I am. And I can do a lot of cool things, and a few not so cool things, but I don't know how to hack into things and bypass passwords and all that."

"What about that stuff you got back at the library?"

"I didn't hack into anything for all that. It was just out there. I know how to find things that are public record or floating into cyberspace that are free for the taking but that's about it. I'm not a hacker. I'm a graphic designer."

"Isn't it close to the same?" Hall jokingly asked, though it wasn't plainly evident in his serious tone.

"No!"

"Well we gotta think of something or we'll just spin our wheels most of the day and waste the day away."

Charlotte didn't want to even entertain that possibility. In order to get this thing over with, she'd do just about anything. Including interacting with a former boyfriend. She closed her eyes and ever so slightly shook her head, not believing what she was about to suggest. She opened her eyes and stared out the front windshield, giving it some extra thought.

"I have an idea," she finally blurted out.

Hall turned his head and looked at her strangely since she said it in an unusual manner. "OK? What is it?"

Charlotte let out a sigh, taking a few extra seconds to make sure it was what she really wanted. "I think I know someone that can help."

"Really? Who?"

"My, uh, ex-boyfriend."

Hall could tell by her voice shaking that she was extremely uncomfortable in saying that. Whatever the problem was, he could tell that it was a major issue for her.

"Your ex?"

Charlotte let out another deep breath, then ran her hand over her face, not liking the scenario one bit. Hall could see that she was in deep discomfort just thinking about it. But as much as he'd appreciate any extra help they could get, he was leery about putting her through something that was obviously awkward for her and giving her an anxiety attack.

"I'm assuming there's some bad history there?"

Charlotte snapped her head toward him and stared at him, her eyes looking like daggers that might jump out and stab him at the mere mention of her ex. "Why do you say that?"

Hall quickly realized he had to tread carefully with the subject. "Umm, probably because it looks like you're about to go all psycho killer on me right now just for asking about it?"

Feeling bad that she looked so hostile to him, Charlotte quickly dropped her stare, letting her eyes fall to the console between them. "I'm sorry, I didn't mean to. It's just... there's a lot of history there."

"Hey, if it's a problem for you, we don't have to go. It's no big deal. We can find another way, that's all. Don't worry about it."

Charlotte rubbed her eyes, not yet close to crying, but a sense of sadness overcoming her as she thought about her ex.

"No, I have to get through this and finally get him out of my system. They say you always have to confront your fears or what you feel is holding you back to finally get over it and move on, right?"

"Uh, yeah, sure."

"Well, he's the only person I know of that can do this... and do it fast, so that's what we'll have to do."

"Your ex-boyfriend can hack into websites?"

Charlotte rolled her eyes, almost embarrassed to admit she dated someone like that. "Yeah."

"Umm, I have like a ton of questions, but I should probably hold off on them, shouldn't I?"

As much as Charlotte didn't like talking about her ex, she didn't want anything hanging in the air or wondering what Hall was going to ask. Plus, she didn't want him to ask her ex anything embarrassing once they were there, so she felt it was probably better to get their backstory out of the way ahead of time.

"Just ask it. It's better that you know now instead of

later, so just ask away."

"So how did you wind up with a computer hacker?" Hall asked.

Charlotte was already aggravated and figured it was better to just tell her story without being pestered with a bunch of little questions.

"OK, I'll just tell you about him and get it out in the open."

"Uh, OK," Hall said. He was starting to get uncomfortable about the whole situation before even hearing anything about it.

"So I met Corey in college and we really hit it off."

"Nice."

"No smart remarks." Hall just lifted his arms in the air to indicate he would comply. "Anyway, he was into that stuff even then, but I was kind of going through a rebellious side of my own, so I really didn't pay it much attention."

"You were a rebellious college kid?"

"I wasn't disrespectful or mean to anybody, it was just a state of mind really... enough about that though."

"Are you sure?"

"Shut up," she playfully said. "Anyway, it got really serious, and we dated for a few years and eventually he asked me to marry him."

Hall looked at her hand. "I'm assuming that didn't go very well."

"I said yes because I was really happy while I was

with him."

"So what happened?"

"I found out that he'd been cheating on me the whole time," Charlotte answered. "Almost the entire time we were together, he had someone on the side."

Hall just looked down and shook his head, feeling bad for her. "I'm sorry."

"I couldn't believe it. I was just... in so much shock and pain."

"That's terrible."

"So I flushed his ring down the toilet and threw him out of our apartment," Charlotte said, dabbing at her eyes to try to hold back the tears that so desperately wanted to come out. She tried to flash a smile to make it seem like it didn't still hurt, even though it did. "That was two years ago. That's when I moved to the apartment I have now. Figured it'd be a new start."

Hall reached over and put his hand on her shoulder and rubbed it, trying to comfort her. "It's OK. We can find another way."

Charlotte wiped her face and flashed him a real smile this time. "No, it's fine. Like I said, he can really help us, and I think it's what I really need. To face him one more time. If only so I can slap him."

"Well wait until he actually helps us before you do that."

Charlotte laughed. "OK."

"Have you seen or talked to him since then?"

"Not in person. He sent me a few text messages

after I threw him out but that was it."

"How'd you actually find out he was doing that stuff?" Hall asked.

"Why? You want pointers?"

Hall snickered. "No, I would never do that. I believe that if you're going to cheat on a person, then you obviously don't want to be with them, so you should just break up with them first."

"Good call. But anyway, a friend of mine saw him out to dinner with another woman, when he was supposed to be visiting his parents. My friend took his picture so I'd have proof."

"So you confronted him with it?"

"Not at first. First, I started snooping through his phone and computer, which I never do. I believe people deserve their privacy, so I'm not one of those people who is constantly checking on their significant other's history. I trust people until I'm given a reason not to."

"So I take it you found a lot of other stuff?"

"Oh yeah. You could only get on his computer with a password, so one night I snuck up behind him as he was typing it in so I could see what it was. Then the next time he left, I went on it. He's such a weasel."

"So you really wanna do this?"

"I don't know if I really want to, but we need to."

"Are you sure he'll actually help us?"

"Oh, he'll help," Charlotte replied. "If he knows what's good for him... he'll help."

14

It was a half an hour drive to get to Charlotte's ex-boyfriend's house. It was actually a two bed, two bath condo that was on the third floor of a large building that used to be an industrial sized warehouse before it was converted to a residential complex. Charlotte saw his car in its assigned parking spot, so she knew he was there. But she knew he'd probably be there anyway, since he spent most of his day working on his craft.

Although Corey's initial ambition, at least when Charlotte met him, was to be a computer programmer and design video games, his excellent computer skills were usually a detriment to him. Too often he got sucked into the wrong kind of crowd, and even though Charlotte knew that really wasn't the kind of person he was, he was never strong enough to resist the temptation of making a quick buck here and there. Even though he did a few illegal things from time to time when they were together, Charlotte always thought she could straighten him out. Corey still dabbled in designing games from time to time, but it seemed as though that dream was a distant memory. She always figured if she kept on him long enough, he'd eventually get back to that guy she first met and was attracted to, but it never happened. At least not while they were together. Most of his time nowadays centered on how to make him more money. He enjoyed not working a regular nine-to-five job. He enjoyed spending money on fancy dinners and buying gifts to impress women. He was never going back to the struggling world of game design. Not when it was easier to do something illegal for some fast cash.

As Hall and Charlotte got out of the car and walked to the entrance of the building, something struck him as funny. Before actually reaching the door, Hall grabbed her by the arm to stop her progress.

"Hey, I just thought of something."

"Hopefully it's something useful," Charlotte quipped.

"No, I mean, yeah... what I mean is... how'd you know this guy lives here?"

Charlotte looked at him strangely. "What do you mean?"

"You said you haven't talked to him in two years, didn't you?"

"Yeah?"

"So how'd you know this is where he lives?"

Charlotte rolled her eyes and sighed, knowing she'd been caught. "OK, maybe we texted a few times after I dumped him."

"Maybe?"

"OK, so he texted me a few months later and asked what I was up to and invited me over to this new place that he was renting."

"This one?" Hall asked.

"Yeah."

"So'd you go?"

An uncomfortable look came over Charlotte's face as her body started contorting, trying not to answer the question.

"You did go, didn't you?" Hall said.

"I just came for like an hour to see how he was and if he'd changed or anything?"

"And?"

"He was still the same obnoxious prick that I threw out of my apartment."

"OK?" Hall said, assuming there was more to the story.

"OK, what?"

"Well that was how long ago? Year and a half?"

"So?"

"Year and a half's a long time to assume someone's staying at the same place. How'd you know he was still here now?"

Charlotte shrugged her shoulders. "Just took a wild guess?"

Hall wasn't buying it though. He just shook his head at her. "You've passed by here from time to time, haven't you? Seeing if his car's still here? Maybe sitting in the parking lot to see if he's hanging out with other women? Huh? Am I right?"

Charlotte immediately got defensive. "No, you're not right!"

"About which part?"

"All of it!"

"Oh really?"

"Yes, really."

"So how'd you know he was still here?"

"I just assumed that he was."

Hall raised an eyebrow, not believing it. "I'm not buying it."

"Well I don't care what you're buying."

"I'm not going in until you tell me the truth."

"Why? What's it matter to you?" Charlotte asked.

"What was it you said? You gotta face your fears in order to move on or something like that? Isn't truth and honesty and looking at yourself in the mirror a part of all that?"

Charlotte looked at him with contempt, not because of what he was saying, but because he was right. And she didn't like to admit it. After letting it sink in for a minute, her scornful expression faded away.

"Fine, you're right."

"What was that?" Hall said, putting his hand up to his ear, pretending that he didn't hear her.

Charlotte moved her jaw around, rolling her tongue from side to side inside her mouth. She could tell Hall was having fun. "You enjoying yourself?"

"Eh, maybe just a little. What was it you said again?"

"I said, fine, you're right."

Hall then let out a laugh. "Oh, that's what you said."

"You know I really don't like you sometimes." Hall smiled, knowing she really didn't mean it.

"So which part was true? All of it?"

"No! Only some of it." Hall raised an eyebrow again, expressing doubt on her story. "Fine, if you must know, I drove by every now and then, not on purpose, but I happened to see his car when I did."

"Just happened to, huh?"

"Yes. Is that OK with you?"

"So you didn't sit in the parking lot and watch?"

"No!" After receiving another glance from Hall, she doubled down on her story. "OK, fine, you win. From time to time I drove by to see if he was still there, but at no point did I ever sit in the parking lot and watch him move. I mean, maybe it's pathetic to do what I did, but I'm not that much of a loser."

Hall smiled at her, glad to have her finally spill the truth. "I don't think you're a loser or pathetic."

Charlotte glared at him, thinking he was just trying to be nice. "Really?" she said, a flare of attitude evident behind her voice.

"No, seriously, I don't. Hey, you had a long-term relationship, you loved the guy, you got hurt, I get it. Sometimes it's hard to move on. Sometimes it's hard to accept things. It's hard to throw a few years away right down the toilet."

"Yeah, well, I'm over it now."

As Hall gave her a look, Charlotte didn't want to go into it any further. She grabbed hold of his arm and led him into the lobby of the building. It was a five-floor building, so they took the elevator up to the third floor. With Charlotte leading the way, they quickly found the door with the golden 306 numbers on it. Once they did, they just stood there in front of the door for a minute. Hall figured he'd let Charlotte take charge, but as he looked over at her, she looked a little nervous.

"You need, like, one of those bags to throw up in or something?"

Charlotte took another deep breath. "No. Let's just get this over with."

She somehow got her arm to move and brought it up to the door, knocking loudly three times. A minute later, after hearing some shuffling around inside, they heard someone hurrying to the door. Once it opened, they saw Corey standing there, him and Charlotte just staring at each other. Neither could quite believe that the other one was standing right in front of them.

For Hall, he could hardly believe that Charlotte saw anything in that guy. At least from Hall's initial impression, he didn't appear to be anyone worth getting hung up over. It looked like he hadn't shaved in a week or two judging by his scruffy face. His thick hair was messed up and looked like it hadn't been combed in a while. And he appeared to either be high or hung over, although judging by the whiff of alcohol Hall was smelling, he guessed it was the latter.

"Uh, hey," Corey said, taking a glance at Hall before focusing back on Charlotte. "What, uh, what are you doing here?"

Charlotte huffed before answering. "We need a favor."

Corey took another view of Hall, a little leery of him. "What's up? What do you need?"

Charlotte could barely believe what she was about to say, considering she was always on him to give it up. "We need your skills. We need you to hack into some stuff."

Corey's eyes almost popped out of his head as it lunged forward. He thought he might have drank more than he thought since he was now hearing things. "You need what?"

Charlotte looked at Hall, not really wanting to repeat herself. "We need you to hack into something."

"OOK. Who's we?"

Charlotte pointed to Hall and herself. "We. Us."

"And who's that?" Corey asked, looking at Hall again. "Who's he?"

Hall was about to answer for himself, but Charlotte quickly interrupted him before he was able to get a word out. "Oh, this is Brandon. He's my boyfriend."

An uneasy feeling came over Charlotte, not knowing why she said that, considering she hadn't planned on introducing Hall that way. She had initially planned to just say that he was a friend. But maybe, upon finally seeing Corey again, she wanted to somehow make him jealous. Or maybe she just wanted to make it seem like she was more over their previous relationship than she let on. Whatever the case was, she just blurted it out without thinking. Hall just slowly turned his head, almost like he was in slow motion, to look at his apparent new girlfriend. Charlotte could feel his stare and returned a look of her own, flexing muscles in her face and jaw, hoping that he didn't say otherwise. Hall could tell by her face, though, that this was pretty important to her, so he just went with it. He then looked at Corey and just smiled.

Corey nodded his head a few times, still not seeing why they would need him. "So what do you need me for?"

"We need you to hack into a train passenger list so we can find, uh...," Charlotte said, struggling to find the words for who they were after. "A smuggler?"

"A smuggler?" Corey said with a laugh, thinking he was being put on. "What's he smuggling? Diamonds?"

"Could be," Hall replied, his face deadly serious.

The happy look on Corey's face was now gone as he looked the two of them over. "Wait, you're serious?" He only got a nod from Charlotte to indicate that they were. "You're actually serious?"

"There are several criminal elements at play here, with a bunch of bad actors, and we need to identify exactly who we're dealing with," Hall said, sounding like he was an intimidating FBI agent or something.

His tone wasn't lost on Corey, who now suspected his ex's new boyfriend worked for the police. He immediately looked to Charlotte for answers.

"Wait, is he a cop or something? Did you bring the heat down on me?"

"No, he's not a cop."

"Then what's really going on?"

Hall and Charlotte looked at each other, neither sure at first whether they should just tell the truth, or say something that sounded good without informing Corey of the exact details. Hall figured it was better to just come out with it.

"I just got out of the military a little while ago. I was on a train yesterday when I was attacked by a group of men thinking I was some kind of criminal carrying their merchandise. After I escaped from the train, I went to my apartment, where they then had men waiting for me there."

"What are you? Some type of Rambo or something? Taking people out at different locations all over the city?"

"Can you help or not?" Charlotte impatiently asked.

"I dunno. What do you guys need exactly?"

"We're thinking the real person they were after was on that train. Someone else tried to help them get away by picking my name out of a hat so they'd come after me. While I was keeping them busy, the real person with the merchandise was able to get away."

"So what are you looking for?" Corey asked. "To find this other person on the train? Assuming there is such a person."

"Yep."

"I dunno, man, that seems like...." Corey was about to say no, not really interested in helping. But then he looked at Charlotte, who looked like fire was about to shoot out of her eyes at him. She looked angry. Even though he hadn't changed his ways any since they split up, Corey still felt a little bad about how their relationship ended. He didn't feel he owed her anything, but maybe out of some small semblance of guilt, decided he would help them out after all.

"All right, all right, come in," Corey said, opening the door fully for his guests to enter.

As soon as they entered, Hall was immediately struck by the big desk in the corner of the room. It was a huge L-shaped desk that housed eight computers, an even mix between desktops and laptops.

"You just get up or something?" Charlotte asked, noting her ex's disheveled appearance.

"Uh, I dunno, a little while ago I guess."

A scantily clad woman appeared from the bedroom, wearing a tank top that looked to be a few sizes too small, as her large breasts were popping out of it. She also was only wearing thong underwear, and didn't seem to be the least bit embarrassed that strangers were in the house. Hall and Charlotte both turned their heads and stared at her. But Charlotte wasn't mad or jealous. In fact, her mind immediately went to Hall, hoping he wasn't gushing over the woman. After a few seconds, Charlotte's head snapped back to Hall, to see if he was looking. Hall took his eyes off the pretty woman and looked at Charlotte, as he could feel her gazing at him. He took a gulp, then turned his attention back to Corey, who was at his computer station and wasn't paying anything much mind.

"Hey, babe, who are these people?" the woman asked.

"Oh, just, uh, that's an... they're just people I'm helping for something."

"Oh. Well hi."

"Go back to bed. I'll be in in a little bit."

She flashed Hall a seductive smile and waved at him. Hall, still feeling the heat of Charlotte's stare, just faked a smile, then glanced at his supposed girlfriend.

Once Corey sat down and had all his equipment on, he started asking questions.

"OK, so I need as much information as you can give me."

Hall and Charlotte sat down and started saying everything they knew. They revealed the names of all the players involved, the addresses of the businesses they owned, as well as Hall's itinerary, from San Diego until he got off the train at Anaheim. With what they told him, Corey felt he had a good base to work with. Hall was impressed with how fast his fingers moved on the keyboard. After only a few minutes, Corey was already paying dividends.

"I'm in!" Corey said, clapping his hands. Although he wasn't initially interested in helping, once he was involved in something, he couldn't help but feel the rush of hacking into something that he shouldn't be in. It was an exhilarating feeling for him.

"In where?" Charlotte asked. Though she was looking at the screen, she really couldn't tell what he was doing.

"I got the passenger list from the train."

"Great. You able to tell anything yet?"

"Nah, I'm still working on it. I'm going to cross reference everyone who was on the train with those who have a criminal record. I mean, it's likely that whoever they used also has a record, right?"

"Stands to reason," Hall replied.

"So if we get a hit on that, I'd assume it wouldn't be

that big of a list. Then we can check those who have a record to see if they have any connection to Palumbo. I've heard of that guy, man, he's a bad dude. I wouldn't want him on my trail, I'll tell you that. I've heard he's killed a lot of people." Hall and Charlotte just looked at him. Corey then realized he probably said too much and stopped typing for a second. "Sorry."

Corey went back to pounding on the keyboard.

"How long do you think it'll take?" Hall asked.

"Not too long. Probably only a few minutes."

"Really? I thought it'd take hours."

"Nah, man, you just gotta know where to look and how to get the information you need. Once you got that, you just have to break in."

"You seem like you've done this before."

Corey glanced over at them and gave them a wry smile, indicating that he had. Though he was used to getting money for doing it. He gave thought to asking for something in this case too, but considering it was Charlotte, he figured it'd be on the house.

"So how long you two kids been together?" Corey asked. He usually didn't like to work in silence. Most of the time he had the radio on, or headphones listening to music or a podcast, but people chatting in the background would work for him too. Just listening to something, even if he wasn't paying much attention to it, seemed to relax him and help him focus. Silence was like nails on a chalkboard for him. If he worked in complete quiet for hours, it would make him go crazy.

Hall and Charlotte answered his question in complete unison. “Six months,” she said. “A month,” Hall replied.

Corey just looked at the two of them, wondering what their issue was. Charlotte quickly changed her story though.

“What I mean is, we’ve only been together a month, but it already seems like six months since we’ve been through so much together already.”

Charlotte flashed him a big smile, then interlocked her arm with Hall’s, squeezing it affectionately to keep up the charade.

“Well that’s cool,” Corey said. “Shame you got mixed up in all this, but I guess it just goes to show you, bad crap can happen to anybody at any time, right?”

“Yeah,” Hall said.

“So how’d you guys meet?”

“What’s this?” Charlotte replied. “Sixty questions?”

Corey waved his hand near his head, like he was fanning himself. “Just keep throwing stuff at me. You know I always like to have background noise when I’m working. If not, I’ll just... you know, whatever.”

Charlotte looked at Hall, not sure what to say. Hall quickly thought of something, though.

“We just happened to bump into each other,” Hall said, trying to figure out their story on the fly. He eventually decided on something that really wasn’t that far from the truth. “I just got my discharge and was looking for apartments, then I stumbled on a place that was directly across from hers. Just kind of bumped into each other in the hallway. I guess the rest is history, as they say."

Hall playfully put his arm around Charlotte's shoulder and gently squeezed.

"Well that's good. I'm happy for you guys. Hope it lasts a while for you."

"Thanks," Charlotte replied.

Corey stopped typing again to talk to Hall. "I don't know if you know this, but her and I were actually a thing a couple years ago."

"Yeah, I know. And I know what you did to her. You're actually quite lucky that you're helping us right now or else I'd probably kick your ass for hurting her."

Corey's face dropped, worrying that it might still happen. Charlotte put her hand over her mouth to keep from laughing out loud, though she did enjoy the thought. After Corey went back to work, Charlotte turned her head to look at her partner, who simply shrugged at her. Hall wasn't sure why he said what he did, but it really was the truth. He really liked Charlotte, and seeing how this guy hurt her, really got his dander up. But considering the predicament they were in, he was able to control it.

"You know I usually charge money for this," Corey said, beginning to change his mind from his earlier stance. Especially in light of the apparently violent man sitting across from him.

"How about we make a deal?" Hall said. "You don't charge us money and I won't throw you out your third-floor window?"

Corey made an uncomfortable sounding laugh, not really believing that he would do such a violent deed, but also not completely sure he wouldn't either. "You wouldn't really do that."

Hall leaned forward, seemingly taking delight in intimidating the man. It wasn't his usual style, and he was probably only doing it because of Charlotte's past with him, but he couldn't resist in the moment.

"You know, I was in a special ops unit in the marines. While you were learning to do this, I was being trained to kill in over a hundred different ways."

Corey glanced up at him, trying not to pay him much attention. "Uh, good... it's good knowledge to have I guess."

"Yeah. I mean, I've only had to use about thirty-five of them up to this point. Still have a lot of things I'd like to practice on."

Charlotte put her hand over her nose and mouth again, not believing this conversation was happening. She figured they'd have to be extra nice and polite, but Hall was throwing all that right out the window. Not that she was really complaining. She actually was taking some delight in watching her former boyfriend squirm in his seat. It served him right, she thought.

Corey, wanting to hurry up and get them out of his house, started to really up his game. The sooner he had the information they wanted, the quicker they'd be out of his house. And that's what he wanted most at that moment. Afraid of Charlotte's new boyfriend and what he could and might do, he didn't dare ask them to leave before he had what they were looking for.

About twenty minutes passed by, still a bunch of small talk happening between the trio. Corey stopped typing and leaned back in his seat, the small presence of a smile creeping over his lips.

"What is it?" Charlotte asked, recognizing that look. She'd seen it before.

"I've got it down to three."

"Three what?"

"Three guys on that train with criminal records."

"Can you narrow it down further?"

Corey nodded. "Yeah, just give me a few minutes. Looking to see if they have connections to Palumbo."

"How easy will that be?" Hall asked.

Corey shrugged and tossed up his hands from the keyboard, not having any idea. "Could be hard. Could be easy. Guess we'll see."

After a few more minutes of banging away, Corey let out a very loud sigh, indicating he was frustrated by something.

"What is it?" Charlotte asked.

"There's a small problem."

"What?" Hall said.

"I've narrowed it down to two."

"OK? So what's the problem?"

"Problem is that they both have connections to Palumbo."

"Both of them?" Charlotte asked. "How can that be?"

"I don't know. But it's right there in black and white," Corey said, pointing to the screen.

"No, you know what, it makes sense," Hall said. "If Palumbo's smart enough to use one red herring in me, he's smart enough to use two. That way if his plan was discovered, probably thinking it'd be Kowalski, that way he'd spend all his time chasing me, then another guy who doesn't have anything. Just gives the real person all the more time to get away."

"Yeah, that makes a lot of sense."

"So how are we going to figure out which one of the two is it?" Charlotte asked.

Hall turned to Corey. "Are you able to track down each of these guys right now? See where they're at or what they're doing?"

"I can give it a shot."

"And what if he can't?" Charlotte asked.

"Then I guess we'll be paying both of them a visit."

15

Though Corey tried to track down both individuals that had ties to Palumbo, he was only able to get a lead on one. The man in question left an online trail that led Corey to decipher that he was actually on the internet in his condo at that very moment. Hall knew they'd have to move now, while the man was still at his house. Corey wasn't able to get a read on the other man's location and Hall knew they couldn't afford to wait for it.

"We gotta go," Hall said.

"What about the other guy?" Charlotte asked.

"We don't have time to wait. There's no guarantee we'll find the other one, and If this is the guy and we wind up losing him, we'll really be up the creek."

"No, he's right," Corey said. "I'm having a hard time with the other guy, he's not on the grid right now.

Might pop up at some point, but right now, it's not happening."

"How long's the guy been on?"

"Uh, looks like about twenty minutes right now."

Corey gave them the man's address, and Hall and Charlotte popped out of their chairs and headed for the door. Corey followed them over, more excited to finally be rid of them then he was at actually finding anything for them. Hall opened the door, but turned around before he walked out.

"Do me a favor and keep on the other guy for a little while?"

Corey rolled his eyes and moaned and groaned, not really feeling it. As far as he was concerned, he did his duty and was now done with it. Seeing he was trying to weasel his way out of it, Charlotte wasn't about to let that happen.

"Just do it," she forcefully said.

Corey was a little surprised by how authoritative she was and snapped his head back. Reluctantly, he agreed. "All right, fine, I'll give it another hour, tops. But if I can't find nothing on him by then, that's it, he just ain't gonna be found. I got other stuff I need to work on you know."

"One hour," Hall repeated, thinking that was fair.

Before the duo left, Corey and Charlotte locked eyes one more time. Corey smiled at her and put his arms out, wanting a final embrace. "One more hug for old time's sake?"

Charlotte smiled and tilted her head, thinking there was no way on this earth that she was going to hug him again. Still, she took a few steps toward him, making her former boyfriend think she was going to oblige him. Just before they touched each other, Charlotte brought her right hand back, then uncorked a wicked and powerful open-handed slap to the side of Corey's face.

"Damn," Hall said, enjoying the moment.

With Corey not suspecting the attack at all, he was instantly dropped, falling to his knees.

"I've been waiting a long time for that," Charlotte said. "Probably should've done it the last time I saw you, but maybe the wait makes it sweeter. If you want to hug somebody, go hug that floozy of yours."

Corey held the side of his face, feeling like he just got decked by a professional boxer. He rubbed his cheek as he looked up at his former girlfriend. Though he wasn't exactly thrilled with being hit, he found it hard to be mad. He supposed he had it coming. Even if he was angry about it, he wouldn't do anything about it. Not with Hall being there. Corey wasn't brave enough to tangle with him. At least not in a fistfight.

Charlotte stayed put for a few moments, kind of proud of what she just did. She certainly did get some enjoyment out of it. "Don't forget. One hour. We better get a report. If you decide to slack off or jerk us around, I'll send him back here to talk to you."

Corey fearfully looked at Hall, who was just

standing there with his arms crossed. "Yeah, yeah, I got it. I'll call you."

As they rode the elevator down to the first floor, Hall could tell Charlotte was still a little worked up. Her hands were shaking, and she was breathing heavily.

"You really gave it to him good," Hall said.

Charlotte rubbed her arms, now a little awkward about the incident. "I don't know what came over me up there."

"It's nothing to be embarrassed about. You had a right to do it. It was a long time coming."

"I don't know if I did or not, but I feel different somehow."

"Maybe it's what you needed to take the load off your shoulders."

"Yeah, maybe. Oh, and uh, thanks for playing the part of my new boyfriend back there."

Hall looked at her and smiled. "It's OK. I kind of enjoyed it."

"I've never done anything like that before."

Hall scrunched his eyebrows together, wondering what she was talking about. She must have had a really short memory, because he distinctly remembered her going to town on a few guys in her apartment.

"Umm, what about...?" Hall said, pointing to his right hand, which was mimicking her motion of beating the guys in her apartment with the frying pan.

"Oh, well I meant before I met you and all." Charlotte thought about all the excitement brought into her life since she met Hall. "Maybe it's you. Maybe you're bad luck or something."

"Me?"

"Well you have to admit, ever since I met you, things have been happening left and right."

Hall just shrugged. There wasn't much he could say. He couldn't really deny it. A few seconds later the elevator door opened, and the two of them sprinted out of the building to their car. It was roughly a twenty-minute drive to get to the house of Jayson Wendel. Hall thought he could make it in fifteen though if he stepped on the gas a little.

"You really think this guy's who we're looking for?" Charlotte asked as Hall sped around some slower cars.

"I don't know. Guess we'll find out when we get there."

"I don't think it is."

"Why not?"

"If this guy's really the guy, you really think he'd be spending his time right now surfing the internet?"

"Maybe he's waiting on something. Maybe an exchange doesn't go down for a couple hours. It's tough to say."

"I mean, I hope he is," Charlotte said. "I just don't get a good feeling about it."

"Like I said, we'll see when we get there."

"What are you going to do? Break his door down? I

was listening when you said you were trained to do that."

"Yeah, I was hoping to take him in a little different fashion this time," Hall replied. "Maybe catch him more by surprise."

"What's more surprising than seeing your door falling over?"

Hall laughed. "You know, probably not much. But if he's not in the same room when the door caves in, that probably gives him a few seconds to prepare himself. I'd rather not give him that time."

"What's that leave?" Charlotte asked. "Drop in through the ceiling? Jump through the window? Somehow rise through the floor?"

"That would be a cool trick, coming up through the floor."

"I'd pay to see it."

"I had something a little simpler in mind."

"What?"

"Just knock," Hall answered.

"Oh. You really think that will work?"

"Why not?"

"Well what if your face has been distributed to all of Palumbo's cronies by now? I'm sure he's not going to just open the door without checking to see who it is first. And considering he doesn't know you, I kind of have my doubts as to whether he's actually going to open it for you."

"I agree."

Now Charlotte looked confused. "Wait, if you agree, then why are you going to do it."

"I didn't say I was gonna do it."

"You just said you were going to knock."

"No, I said my plan was to knock. I didn't say it was gonna be me."

It didn't take a whole lot of thinking for Charlotte to know who he was referring to. Considering they were a two-person team at the moment, there could only be one other option.

"Why does it have to be me?"

"You said it yourself," Hall replied. "He's probably not going to open the door for me. I look too threatening. And if you're right, and he does know my face, then he's probably just gonna shoot me through the door."

"Oh, so I'm the one that has to take the bullet?"

"He's not gonna shoot you."

"How do you know?"

"Because he doesn't have a reason to."

"What if they know my face too?" Charlotte asked.

"I don't think they've had time for all that. I was planned. You're a wild card."

"But... why's it gotta be me?"

"There's really no one else I can ask."

"Can't you just jump through a window instead? It'd be a whole lot more fun for you."

Hall smiled, their idea of fun differing. "You can do it."

"What am I supposed to do?"

"Just knock. I'll take care of the rest."

"What should I say if he opens the door?"

"How about... hi?"

"And then what?" Charlotte asked.

"That's it. Just need him to open the door. Once he does that, I'll go to work."

"OK, but what if he's not by himself? What if the other guy is with him?"

"Then head to the kitchen for a frying pan."

"You're never gonna let me live that down, are you?"

Hall shook his head. "Not likely."

"I thought so. And what if he doesn't open the door? What if he just asks me what I want without opening it?"

"Make up a good reason why he'll need to."

"And if that fails?"

"Then we'll go to Plan B."

"Which is what?"

"I guess I'd have to break the door down."

"Ooh, I like that plan a lot better."

"We'll only do that as a last resort," Hall said.

"I don't really want to do this. I'm not cut out for this kind of stuff."

"Your actions say otherwise. But listen, if you're really not comfortable doing it, it's fine, I won't make you. I'll find another way."

Charlotte didn't immediately reply, thinking about

their options. Not that they really had many. This really was the next logical step. "No, I'll do it."

"Are you sure? Because you really don't have to if you'd rather not."

"Well I would rather not, but I'll do it, anyway."

"I'll be right there next to you the whole time," Hall said, hoping that would reassure her a bit. "I'll just be out of his line of sight."

"You probably don't want to hear this, but I really hope he doesn't answer the door."

"He will."

"Why are you so certain?"

"Because he's a man and you're a pretty woman," Hall replied.

"So?"

Hall looked at her strangely, not believing that she didn't know what he was talking about. "You really need me to spell it out for you?"

"Uh, yeah, I guess so?"

"If a pretty woman shows up at a man's door for something, he's probably gonna answer thinking he might get lucky, eventually. If not that day, then at some other time."

"What?" Charlotte asked, thinking that was the most ridiculous thing she'd ever heard. "No guy is going to think he's gonna get laid just because a woman knocks on his door."

"Believe me, Charlotte, not all men are that intelligent. And when a pretty woman shows up, sometimes intelligent thinking goes right out the window. Especially when they start thinking with the wrong body parts."

"That's just gross. And I'm not even that pretty. Maybe he prefers redheads."

"Just trust me. He's going to answer."

16

The entire ride over to Wendel's condo, Charlotte was hoping something else would come into Hall's mind, something bigger and better than the plan he had. Not that she thought it was a bad plan, she just didn't like being the main player in it. By the time they got there, in fifteen minutes, she looked over at him, hoping he was about to let loose with this new, alternative plan. He didn't though.

"Ready to do this?" Hall said.

Charlotte curled her upper lip, unhappy with his question. "I suppose."

"Like I said, you don't have to go through with it if you're really uncomfortable."

"No, let's just hurry up and do this before I change my mind."

Charlotte's fingers had just reached the handle of

the door, but she quickly turned her head back to Hall when she felt the touch of his hand on her forearm.

"Everything's going to be fine," Hall said. "Believe me, I would never intentionally put you in a spot that I thought would be dangerous. If I thought there was even an ounce of potential of you getting hurt, I would do it myself."

Charlotte gave him a warm smile. "I know."

They got out of the car, but before finding Wendel's place, Charlotte made a call to Corey, wanting to make sure that their target was actually still there. There was no point in going there and wasting their time if he'd already flown the coop. Luckily, Corey could confirm that he was still there, as the man had checked some of his social media pages only a few minutes before the call.

Wendel's unit was right in the middle of an eight block group of homes. Before going toward the door, Hall looked at his partner, just to make sure she could go through with it. She looked back at him and took a deep breath, not saying a word or making any other type of motion. She swallowed her nerves and quickly hurried to the door before she lost her gumption. Hall crouched down and ran over to a small bush to the side of the door and hid behind it.

Charlotte put her hand up to knock on the door, but stopped mid-stream, just holding her fist in the air, inches from the dark brown wood. She then willed her hand forward, loudly knocking on the door. She waited about twenty seconds but no one answered. She then knocked again. A few seconds later, a voice emerged from behind the door.

"What do you want?"

"Oh, um," Charlotte wasn't sure what to say and quickly improvised. She stuck her hand in her pocket and removed her phone, holding it up in the air. "This is kind of embarrassing. I'm new in the neighborhood, and I'm renting out one of the units behind you, and my phone just died, and I haven't had a chance to go shopping yet, and I'm hungry, and I just wanted to order a pizza. Is there any way you have a charger I could borrow for my phone, even if it's just for five minutes?"

As soon as she stopped talking, Charlotte just wanted to cringe, thinking there was no way he was going to buy that. It even sounded ridiculous to her. She knew she had to keep a straight face though, as she figured Wendel, assuming that's who she was actually talking to, was probably looking at her. But she still couldn't believe she didn't say something that sounded a lot better than that. She waited for a few seconds, but without getting a reply, was getting anxious. She didn't think the man was buying her story.

Charlotte was just about ready to turn to Hall for further directions when she heard the door unlocking. The door opened a slither, just enough for Charlotte to see half of the man's face. She still tried to deliver one of her warm smiles, but it came out kind of awkward looking. Regardless, the man opened the door and wasn't shutting it, so it seemed to do the trick.

"Hi," Charlotte said in as friendly a tone as she could muster.

The man was acting nervously, looking beyond the pretty woman in front of him, almost expecting someone else to be with her. He actually seemed more nervous than she was, as hard as that was to imagine. Hall crouched down even further, as low as he could get, to make sure he wasn't seen. After not seeing anyone else nearby, the man seemed to relax, opening the door a little wider. He finally let his eyes focus on Charlotte's face, liking what he was seeing.

"So do you have one?" Charlotte asked.

"Have one? Oh, the charger. Yeah, I do. Come on in."

"Thanks so much. You're a real lifesaver."

Charlotte stepped into the house, just waiting for Hall to come crashing in. He wasn't coming yet though, and she struggled as to what to do next. She stepped a little further in, then acted like she was being forgetful, putting her hand on her head.

"Oh, I'm sorry, I forgot to introduce myself, I'm Cha... Charlene."

"Beautiful name. I'm Jayson."

The two shook hands, though Charlotte just wanted to bathe her hand in a sink full of soap for the next hour, feeling grimy.

"I'll tell you what, why don't you let your phone charge here for an hour or two? I'll call for a pizza and we can have dinner together here and get to know each other."

"Wouldn't your girlfriend mind?"

"I'm single."

Charlotte uncomfortably smiled, letting out an even more uncomfortable laugh, wondering what was taking her partner so long. "Oh. Well this must be my lucky day, to run into a single, handsome man like yourself."

"What do you say? Have dinner here? Never know where it might lead."

"Oh, well, you certainly don't beat around the bush, do you?"

Wendel shrugged, a wicked kind of smile plastered on his face, hoping he might get lucky at some point. "Why bother? We're both two attractive people."

She could barely contain herself at this point. She really felt like throwing up in her mouth, having to pretend that she was attracted to the man. Wendel really wasn't a terrible-looking guy, in his thirties, average physique, but knowing he was part of the deal to hurt Hall made him look like a monster in Charlotte's eyes. Though if Hall didn't hurry up, she might have changed that opinion soon.

Just as Charlotte was about to feel sick to her stomach, Hall came thumping through the opened door, wrapping his arms around Wendel as the two of them violently crashed onto the floor.

Charlotte quickly moved out of the way. "Thank God. Took you long enough."

Completely caught by surprise, Wendel didn't stand a chance against his hard-hitting opponent. With Wendel's back against the floor, Hall straddled over top of him, and just started teeing off. He alternated between his left and right hands, pounding away on both sides of Wendel's face. It wasn't even a contest, and Wendel was barely fighting back. After only a minute or two of the assault, Wendel could hardly even put his arms up to try to block the forceful blows. As Hall continued beating on the narrowly conscious man, cuts had now formed on both of Wendel's cheeks, along with his nose. Blood started pouring out of the one side of his mouth.

Charlotte stood there, watching the beating, getting more nervous with each blow that landed. She'd never seen anyone killed in person, and she really didn't want to change that now. But Hall didn't seem to be letting up. Charlotte was getting increasingly worried that Hall was going to kill the man with his bare hands. She wasn't sure she could stop him, but she wasn't going to just stand there and let Hall do something stupid. Killing in self defense was one thing, but this wasn't self defense. The guy didn't even know what was going on.

Charlotte rushed over to the fracas and grabbed

one of Hall's arms to stop the beating. Hall initially resisted, still trying to get free to continue the attack. Charlotte then grabbed hold of his waist and tried to pull him off the man. Still struggling to control him, Charlotte moved around to the front of him, making sure he could see her. She wrapped her arms around him, finally able to get him to stop the beating and stand up.

The look in Hall's eyes actually scared her a bit. He wasn't like that back at the apartment. It was a much different look in his eyes. It was almost as if she wasn't there, like he was looking through her. Charlotte was concerned about his well-being. She didn't like seeing him in this condition.

"Stop," Charlotte said, putting her hands on both sides of his face. "It's OK. It's OK. He's not going anywhere. It's over."

Hall's heart was racing, and he was completely amped up, but hearing Charlotte's soothing voice appeared to calm him down a little. His eyes seemed to turn back to normal as he looked at her face.

Charlotte stepped to the side just a little and stretched her arm out to point to the injured man. "It's over."

Hall was obviously embarrassed by his actions, nodding his head, then hanging it in shame. He breathed heavily again, and Charlotte, still worried about him, put her hands back on his face again.

"It's OK," Charlotte told him. She held his face still,

making sure they looked into each other's eyes. She didn't want him to feel bad or embarrassed. She just wanted him to be normal again.

Charlotte took her hands off his face, and after another minute, Hall's face shifted back to the nice looking one that she knew. As he let out a few deep breaths, Charlotte's concern started dropping. He seemed in control of himself again.

"You OK?"

Hall nodded. "Yeah. I'm good."

"You sure?"

"Yeah," Hall said, trying to give her one of those warm smiles that he liked about her so much.

"You scared me for a second."

"I'm sorry."

"You don't have to be. What happened?"

Hall shook his head, knowing exactly what happened, but not really wanting to say. It'd happened to him before. It didn't happen every time he was in a battle, but an equal amount of times than not, he couldn't control himself. He just got locked in some kind of zone and wasn't able to pull himself out of it. It happened in the army more times than he would have liked. It was one of the reasons he wanted to get out. He didn't like that feeling. It was why he wanted to get out and start his own business. He didn't want to ever have to exhibit any type of violence again.

"It just happens sometimes," Hall said. "Sometimes I get started, I get worked up, and I have a hard time stopping. It's almost like I get transported somewhere else and I block out everything else around me."

"But you weren't like that back at the apartment."

"I don't know. I can't explain it. Sometimes I get locked in and sometimes I don't. I don't feel like I have any control over when it happens."

Charlotte grabbed hold of his hand, rubbing the outside of it. "You're sure you're OK?"

Hall looked at her fondly, appreciating her gentle nature. "I'm good. Promise. We should probably see what this guy knows."

Charlotte looked down at Wendel, who still wasn't moving. "Uh, I don't think he's in a talkative mood right now. As a matter of fact, he might not talk again for a month."

"Yeah, I guess I overdid it a little, huh?"

Charlotte held her thumb and index finger about an inch apart. "Just a little."

"I guess we should check around and see if we find anything."

"Oh, before we do that, what took you so long?"

"Had to wait until I was sure he wouldn't see me coming," Hall replied.

"It honestly felt like forever and I was about ready to leave."

"Why? Didn't want to stay and have pizza?"

"Ew, gross. I'd rather you stuck a bunch of nails in my back."

"That doesn't sound pleasant."

"Yeah, well, neither is having to flirt with this guy. You should try it next time."

"I'll pass."

"I feel like I need to take a shower now. Feels disgusting."

"Well, you check his bedroom, and I'll stay out here in case he starts moving around."

"Seriously?" Charlotte asked, not thrilled with the prospect of snooping through the man's personal items.

"What's the matter?"

"It's bad enough I had to flirt with him, now I gotta check his underwear drawers and stuff?"

Hall laughed. "Unless you wanna stay out here and babysit?"

That didn't appeal much to her either so she reluctantly went into Wendel's bedroom. "What exactly am I looking for?"

"I don't know. Anything that looks like it might pertain to us. Anything with Palumbo's name, the train, me, a big deal, you know, something like that."

Hall wasn't going to just sit there and let Charlotte do all the work though. He started looking through the living room, while still keeping an eye on Wendel. He checked a few drawers and tables in the room, but there were no papers of interest. Hall then went into the kitchen and opened every drawer and cabinet, even checking the refrigerator and freezer, just in case

Wendel decided to get cute in hiding something. Still Hall found nothing though.

"You all right in there?" Hall asked, walking out of the kitchen. He didn't get a reply, which concerned him a little, so he walked into the bedroom. He took a look back at Wendel, then saw Charlotte sitting on the edge of the bed, her back to him. "You OK?"

Charlotte spun her head around. "Oh, yeah, sorry. I was just looking at these." She held up a bunch of papers in her hand, then got up and walked toward Hall.

"Anything interesting?"

"Not as far as I can tell."

The two walked back into the living room, each taking a few papers to look through. Charlotte sat down in a chair to look through hers, while Hall continued to stand. Neither found anything that looked like it was related to them though.

"Nothing," Hall said in frustration, tossing the papers down on the floor.

"What did you expect?"

"Nothing I guess. More just hoping."

"So what now?"

"He's gonna start talking."

Charlotte looked at Wendel, who still wasn't moving. "Uh, that guy isn't talking to anybody. He'll be lucky if he can eat through a straw for the next year."

Hall went into the kitchen and grabbed a glass, then filled it with water. He came storming out of the kitchen and dumped it over Wendel's face. Wendel coughed a couple times and started moving around as he started to wake up. Hall readied himself in case the man wanted a second go-around. Wendel turned over and got up on his hands and knees as he took a few deep breaths. He stumbled to his feet and held his head, feeling like he got hit by a truck.

"Unless you want more of where that came from, sit over there," Hall said, directing him to a nearby chair.

Wendel stared at him for a few seconds, contemplating whether he wanted to try Hall on again. He basically got jumped the first time and didn't have much of an opportunity to defend himself. He thought in a fair fight, the result might be different the second time around. But after thinking it over, Wendel decided against it. He was already hurting bad and didn't think he could sustain more injuries after another major fight. Plus, he assumed that they wanted something else from him, other than hurting him, otherwise he probably would have been dead by now. He was alive and wanted to remain that way. Wendel staggered over to the chair and plopped himself down, waiting to see what they wanted.

"I know you work for Palumbo," Hall said.

"Who?"

"Listen, this is not an avenue you wanna go down. I'm not the least bit interested in you. If you tell me what I want to know, we'll be out of your hair forever and you'll never have to worry about us again."

"And if I don't?"

"Then the first beating I gave you will just be a warmup. It's also likely that the only way you'll leave this place is in a body bag," Hall said, patting his pocket like he had a gun in there. He wouldn't have gone through with his threat, but Wendel didn't know that. Wendel had to take the man at his word. Considering Hall's prowess with his fists, Wendel figured he was willing to up the stakes a notch if he had to.

"Yo, if I tell you anything about Palumbo or his business, I'm as good as dead anyway."

"Anything you tell us will be kept between ourselves," Charlotte said.

"That's right," Hall said. "Nothing said here will leave this room."

Wendel snickered, not believing them. "I mean, really, let's be real here. Whatever information I give you, you're gonna go run with it, and if you do something against Palumbo, he's gonna know the info came from somewhere. And guess who's doorstep he's gonna come knocking on? Yeah, mine."

"OK, let me rephrase this another way. I don't even care about Palumbo's business, except with how it pertains to me."

"Dude, I don't even know who you are, man."

"My name's Brandon Hall. That mean anything to you?"

Wendel shrugged, never hearing his name before. "You could tell me you're Ronald McDonald and it wouldn't mean nothing."

"OK, this is already starting to get a little old, and you better start answering questions in a way I'd like, or I'm just gonna say I'm done with you."

Charlotte, not sure whether Hall would actually start beating on the man again or not, pleaded with Wendel to start talking. "Please don't make me have to see him doing that to you again. Just tell us what we want to know so we can be out of here."

"I'll tell you how this goes, then you fill in the missing pieces," Hall said. "I was on a train from San Diego yesterday when I was confronted by Rex Kowalski and his cronies. You know him?"

Wendel rolled his eyes, still not wanting to talk, but getting the vibe that bad things would happen to him if he didn't. "Yeah, I know him."

"OK, so I had a skirmish with them on the train, then I had another one with them at my apartment."

"So?"

"So they came after me thinking I had some bag full of merchandise for them. Something that I didn't have. And they were told that by Palumbo, who was using me as a diversion."

"That's a good story."

"It gets even better," Hall said. "I've since found out that Palumbo hired two other men to ride that train. One was a decoy, and the other was the person who really did have the bag. So I guess the question is, which one are you?"

Wendel was thinking about lying or just outright denying everything, but the look that Hall was shooting at him was telling him he better come clean. Hall had almost a crazy look in his eyes that suggested he was not to be messed with.

"What exactly do you wanna know?" Wendel asked.

"Your role in all this. Who the other guy is? What's in the bag? Let's start with that."

"And that's it? If I tell you about it, you'll let me go?"

"That's all I wanna know."

Wendel still didn't look pleased about ratting Palumbo out, but knew he really didn't have any alternative. Not if he wanted to live that is.

"OK, I only have limited knowledge of everything."

"Just tell me what you know," Hall said.

"Palumbo hired me for this job last week, told me to get on this train and said I was going to be a decoy. Said nothing would probably happen on the train, but that I might get a visit from Kowalski a few days after that. If he came, I was to deny everything. If he kept pestering, I was to give him a name of some guy Palumbo knows out in Arizona."

"Why? What would he do?"

"Nothing. The idea would be to just keep giving Rex different names and have him chasing his own tail for months. Meanwhile, Palumbo's deal would be long done by the time Rex figured it all out."

"What's in the bag?"

"Beats me. I never was told. Deals with Palumbo are on a need to know basis. If you're not directly involved, you don't need to know."

"Who actually did have the bag?" Hall asked.

"Like I said, that part didn't involve me, so I couldn't tell you. Was never mentioned to me. All I know is the part that I had."

"I already know who the other guy is. His name is Dustin Shafer."

"Dustin Shafer," Wendel said, saying the name like he knew who it was.

"Sound familiar?"

"Yeah, well, I mean I know of him. Don't know him personally."

"What do you know about him?"

"He's got heavy connections with people all over. California, Nevada, Washington, even down in Mexico I've heard."

"Probably using him to broker a deal," Hall said.

"Most likely."

"You know anything about this deal? When it's taking place? Who Shafer is meeting? Where it's happening?"

Wendel shook his head. "Couldn't tell ya anything. Have no idea."

"Is this Shafer part of Palumbo's usual crew?"

"Nah, Shafer's an independent. He may have worked with Palumbo before, not sure, but he's not associated with anyone in particular. He helps put deals together and takes a piece of it."

"You don't know where he's located then?"

"From what I understand he moves around a lot. Travels the country, even the world. I don't think he has a specific spot he puts down roots in. He goes where the money takes him."

It sounded to Hall and Charlotte like Wendel was leveling with them. They didn't think he knew more than what he was telling. It appeared he was just a stooge that Palumbo used as a decoy, nothing more.

"Is there anything else you can tell us about any of this?" Hall asked.

"Nah, told you all I know."

Hall and Charlotte looked at each other, both with sort of a bewildered look on their face, unsure what to do next. The three of them sat there in silence for a minute, Wendel now joining them with a look, uneasy with the quiet room. As Charlotte was about to tell Hall something, her phone rang. It was Corey. She picked up the phone and went out to the kitchen.

"Yeah?"

"I got him," Corey answered.

"Who?"

"The other guy. Shafer."

"What? How?"

"Nevermind that. All you need to know is I picked up his trail."

"Great," Charlotte said. "Where's he at?"

"He just bought a train ticket."

"To where?"

"Sacramento."

"Sacramento? What's he doing there?"

"I dunno," Corey replied. "That's your department. I'm just giving you what I know. The train leaves in one hour. It departs from Anaheim to Los Angeles, then there's a transfer, then off to Sacramento."

"How much time do we have?"

"Leaves in an hour, so if you're gonna get there, you need to leave lickety-split. According to the train website, it's forty-five minutes from Anaheim to LA, then the transfer takes about one hour and twenty minutes, then it's a long ride to Sacramento."

"All right, thanks."

"Hold up."

"What?"

"I even found a picture of him. I'll send it your way."

"Thanks," Charlotte hurriedly said.

She ran out of the kitchen to tell Hall the news, who could tell by her actions that something big was up.

"We gotta go," Charlotte said.

"Why?"

"I'll tell you on the way, let's go."

Charlotte pulled on Hall's arm, and the two of them flew out of the house. As the two of them got in the car, Hall quickly started the engine and pulled away, even though he had no idea where he was going yet.

"Where to?"

"Train station," Charlotte replied.

"What?"

"Shafer's boarding another train."

"Why?"

"I don't know. Maybe he has a train fetish. Train leaves in one hour to Los Angeles, then off to Sacramento."

"Guess it's time to go hop a train."

17

Hall and Charlotte got back to the train station, just as they were boarding. They immediately went to their seats and remained there until the train departed from the station. A few minutes after the train was in motion, the two of them got up and started walking through the cars, searching for their man. After looking through every car, they still hadn't found Shafer. Unless he was in some type of disguise, he just wasn't there.

"What now?" Charlotte asked.

"Call your boy-toy and have him double check everything?"

"Seriously? Boy-toy? Say that again and I'll wrap this phone around your head."

Hall laughed at how easily she got upset over him. "Noted."

Charlotte called her ex to see if he got his information mixed up. "Hey, we just searched every car, he's not here."

"Hold on, let me check this again," Corey replied.

"You sure he actually boarded?"

"Definitely. His ticket's been validated. He's on that train."

"Well we can't find him. We checked every car."

Corey quickly found out what the problem was. "You can't find him because he's not in a regular seat."

"Where is he?"

"He's got a room. Number six."

"Great. Would've been nice if you told us that before we checked the whole train."

"Listen sister, I'm working for free here, you don't get top of the line service for nothing."

"Brandon might knock you out for free though."

"All right, all right, duly noted. I gave you your info. You should be all set now."

"Good, because if it's not, you'll know who you'll be dealing with again, right?"

"Yeah, yeah, it's good. I'll make sure it's good just so I don't have to deal with you guys again."

"Miss me that much, huh?"

"Seriously Charlotte, when did you become such a big pain in the ass?"

"Only recently."

Charlotte hung up, then passed along the information to Hall.

"You know, you really seem to enjoy taunting him, don't you?"

"I really do, don't I?" Charlotte replied. "I shouldn't, but it really is fun to make him squirm like the weasel he is."

They sat there for a few minutes, deliberately on their next course of action.

"What do we do now? Take him when he gets off the train? Wait until he boards the next one?"

"Can't do that," Hall answered. "It's a long ride to Sacramento. I don't really wanna be a stationary target and take that much time to get off. Plus, it's half a day of just sitting around."

"Well if he gets off this train, there's no guarantee we'll be able to get him privately somewhere. He might stay in a public spot."

"Maybe. I guess that makes it unanimous then. We take him here."

"How?"

Hall just turned his head and gave her a look. She knew what that meant. It was the same look he gave her in the car when he told her about the plan for Wendel.

"Oh no, not again," Charlotte bemoaned, knowing exactly what he was thinking. "I'm not doing that again. You are not going to have me do that again."

"Just one more time."

Charlotte continued shaking her head. "No. No way."

"It'll be so much more effective if it's you."

"Maybe I would consider it if you were on time last time, but you were way late. I mean... way late."

"I promise I'll be faster this time."

Charlotte hunched forward, wanting to pout, whine, and cry at the same time. She put both her hands on her head and deeply sighed, wondering what she did to deserve all this.

"Why does it have to be me again?" she asked in a whiny voice.

"Because you're good at getting men to open doors."

"You're gonna have to do better than that."

"As soon as someone unexpected knocks on his door, Shafer's going to be on guard. If he sees me, his concern is going to be elevated, thinking there's a possible threat."

"And I don't look threatening?"

Hall looked at her sympathetically, wanting to laugh at how she was fighting against it, but made sure he held it inside. "Not particularly, no. You actually seem to do the opposite and break down their defenses, at least if Wendel is any indication."

"I just wanna hide under my bed right now."

Hall wasn't able to control himself any longer and let out a small laugh. "We can wait if you'd prefer not to do it."

Charlotte sighed, knowing it was equally possible that they could wait, and she'd wind up still doing something that really didn't want to. "No, no, I might as well do it now and get it over with before you think of something else to humiliate me with."

Hall wiped away his amused look, grabbing hold of Charlotte's hand and talking more softly. "Listen, same as before, if you're not comfortable, I'm not gonna force you to do something. We can find another way."

Charlotte looked at him and tried to force a smile, though her lips hardly moved. At this point, she just wanted to be done with everything. Right now, she was willing to do just about anything if it meant an end to this whole ordeal. She didn't want to delay it any longer than necessary.

"No, I'll do it. I just want this thing over with."

"So do I," Hall said. "You're sure you're OK with this?"

"Yeah, I'm fine."

Hall looked at the time and saw they had about twenty minutes to go before the train stopped.

"When you wanna do this?" Charlotte asked.

"Wait another five minutes or so. Wanna leave as little time as possible before the train unloads. That way we don't have to worry about subduing him for long."

"One thing though."

"Yeah?"

Since they were still holding hands, Charlotte rubbed his. "Try to keep yourself under control this time. I don't wanna see that out-of-control guy I saw last time."

"I'll try."

They continued holding hands for a few minutes, neither really thinking much of it. They both felt completely comfortable touching and holding each other, almost as if they'd been doing it for years. After five minutes had passed, they looked at each other, making sure they were each ready.

"You ready?" Hall asked.

"Ready as I'll ever be."

They stood up and exited the car they were in and made their way to the private compartments, quickly finding room six. On the way there, Charlotte thought of a plan, wanting to be more prepared in her own mind than she was the last time she did this. As they stood just a few doors away, Charlotte told Hall her plan.

"Once I'm inside, wait a few minutes, then knock."

"What?" Hall asked.

"Let me go inside for a few minutes, then knock."

"No, I'm not doing that. As soon as he opens the door, I'm going in."

"These rooms are not that big," Charlotte said. "If you rush in, there's just as good a chance that I go down as he does. I'd rather not get caught up in everything. Just let me set things up so everything goes off without a hitch."

The look on Hall's face indicated he wasn't thrilled

with her plan. It was a little more than he bargained for. Closing the door once she was inside, meant that he'd lose visual contact with her. That wasn't something he was comfortable with. Seeing that Hall was resisting, Charlotte faced him and put one of her hands on each of his forearms, looking at him in the eye.

"If you want me to do this, just trust me. I know what I'm doing."

"I don't want to send you in there alone," Hall replied, worried about her getting in over her head. "That wasn't what I had in mind. I told you I'm not gonna put you in a dangerous situation. Just get the door open and I'll take over."

"And what if he takes a peek in the hallway and sees you just waiting there? You don't think that's gonna set off alarm bells?"

"I'll just have to take that chance."

"And he could shut the door before you get there. Or pull me inside and take me hostage. Or throw the bag out the window."

"If that bag's as valuable as everyone says it is, he's not throwing it out the window."

Charlotte gave him a stern look. "You know what I'm saying."

Hall knew what she was saying was technically correct, but that didn't mean he had to like it, or go through with it. "I changed my mind, let's just do something else."

Charlotte grabbed a firmer hold of his arms, her fingers digging into his skin. "Brandon, I can do this."

"But you shouldn't have to."

"Just trust me, OK?"

Hall was trying to balance his trust of her versus his obvious concern. In the end, her persistence paid off, as he reluctantly agreed to let her go through with her plan. As they stood there face to face, Charlotte couldn't resist planting a kiss on Hall's cheek. It was as much to keep him calm as it was for her.

"Now wait around the corner for a few minutes, OK?"

Hall nodded, still not liking it a bit. Charlotte released his arms, and he ducked out of sight. With Hall no longer visible, Charlotte took a deep breath, then went over to Shafer's room. She took another breath, not sure how she was actually strong enough to do this, but there she was, knocking on the door before she even knew what she was doing.

Almost right away, a man answered the door. Charlotte immediately recognized Shafer from the picture Corey sent to her. She instantly cringed at his appearance, though not outwardly so, thinking he was even more unpleasant to look at and flirt with than Wendel was.

"Hello there," Charlotte said, flashing a big, beautiful smile.

"Can I help you?" Shafer asked, not a hint of emotion on his face as he seemed all business.

"Umm, no, but I can help you."

"What?" Shafer peeked his head out the door and looked in the hallway to both sides. "Who are you and what do you want?"

"My name is Candy, and I was sent to be your, um, companion for the rest of your trip."

"My companion? Get out of here." Shafer started to close the door, but Charlotte put her arm on it to stop it from closing.

"Wait, wait, wait." Charlotte could see that he wasn't as flirtatious as Wendel was, making her job all the more difficult. "Mr. Palumbo sent me."

"Palumbo? Why?"

Charlotte shrugged, then put her hands on the man's chest, fixing his tie. "I guess he wanted you to be relaxed. He told me to come here and give you whatever you wanted."

Shafer's uptight demeanor finally seemed to relax for a bit. "Is that so?"

"Yes, he didn't tell me specifics, but he said that you'd done a great job so far and he wanted to give you a little extra... bonus."

"I guess that would be you?"

Charlotte gave him a flirty smile, though she felt disgusted as she did it. "I hear it's a long ride wherever we're going."

"Well, we've only got a few minutes until the changeover."

"If you let me in, we could always do something... quickly."

Shafer finally let a grin come over his forty-year-old face. He opened the door further and stepped to the side to allow her to come into his room. As she walked in, he took another peek into the hallway, making sure it wasn't some type of trap. Since no one was there, he felt much better about it. It wasn't what Shafer was expecting, and he was normally all business when he was working, but he certainly couldn't complain about such a nice and pretty surprise.

"So you weren't expecting me?" Charlotte asked, walking all the way toward the window and turning around.

Shafer locked the door, then took a few steps toward his visitor, wanting to get down to some extracurricular activities. He'd only moved about halfway toward her when there was another knock on the door.

"Oh, that should be room service," Charlotte said, hoping to put the man's mind at ease. "I took the liberty of ordering a bottle of wine for us on our journey."

Shafer grinned and turned around. He unlocked the door, still only opening it a little. He was instantly greeted by a closed fist, sending him stumbling backwards, though he never was knocked off his feet. With Shafer temporarily stunned, Hall rushed through the door, closing it behind him as he jumped on top of his opponent before he could regain his wits.

Hall unloaded a few heavy right hands to keep up the pressure, making sure that Shafer could never get in the fight. It wasn't much of a contest though, as Shafer wasn't much of a battler. He was the type of man who was good at brokering deals and moving along the edges. But he wasn't a scrapper. He usually left the fighting to others.

It was a short contest, much like the fight with Wendel. Shafer didn't have much of a chance. Even if he was ready for Hall, he wouldn't have fared well. Even if Shafer had managed to get in a punch or two, Hall would have quickly and easily overwhelmed him due to being the superior fighter. The major difference between the two contests was Hall's behavior. He didn't get locked in that zone that frightened Charlotte so much. Whether it was the location, the fact that Shafer wasn't much of an opponent, or even Charlotte's words beforehand that comforted him, Hall was much more in control of himself this time.

Charlotte worriedly looked on at the mismatch, hoping she wouldn't have to pull Hall off his victim again. Her fears quickly subsided though, seeing Hall slow up on the assault. Knowing he was in complete control, Hall only did what was absolutely necessary. He didn't have to go overboard since Shafer was barely fighting back. He was basically just covering up at this point.

Hall let up on the beating before Shafer was knocked out and picked the man up by his suit jacket. Shafer could hardly stand with the pain he was in, but Hall grabbed him underneath the arms and dragged him over to a chair, sitting him down. Shafer wobbled in the chair as he struggled to keep his balance and not fall over. Hall took a few steps back in order to catch his breath. As he did, he looked at Charlotte and smiled at her, letting her know that he was good. There was nothing to worry about this time.

Shafer dabbed at his nose and mouth, then looked at his hand, observing traces of blood on it. He wearily looked up at his captors, already having an idea of what they wanted, though he hoped he was wrong.

"What do you want?"

"There's a little black bag that you possess," Hall said. "That's what I want."

"I don't know what you're talking about."

Hall looked at Charlotte, so he could continue to stand guard. "Start searching."

Considering they were in a cramped space, it didn't take Charlotte long to find it. It was sitting under a seat, a blanket draped over it to conceal it. Charlotte grabbed the bag and held it up high.

"Guess you missed the elves bring it in," Hall said. Shafer shrugged, not much he could really say. "We're just gonna take it off your hands if that's OK."

"I wouldn't do that if I were you. You have no idea who you're messing with."

"Oh yes I do. No need to tell Palumbo about this, I'll tell him myself."

"You'll be a dead man in twelve hours."

"Yeah, and if you're not out of the country in that time, then so will you."

Shafer looked at him strangely, thinking Hall might have been out of his mind. "You're taking something that doesn't belong to you. And costing myself a lot of money in the process. I don't think you really want to do that. Put the bag back and leave now and I might be persuaded to forget this incident."

Hall was hardly intimidated and didn't really care about any threats levied his way. He'd already been through worse. Hall took the bag from Charlotte and looked inside, seeing the merchandise everyone was fighting over. It certainly looked like it'd be a lot of money.

"You wanna threaten me and think you'll get away with it?" Hall said. He then turned to Charlotte. "Go get an employee and tell him we got a fugitive back here."

"What?" Charlotte asked.

"Just do it. This guy thinks he's gonna be a problem for us. Well I'm gonna make sure he's not a problem for anyone ever again."

As Charlotte left the compartment, Shafer started to shift in his seat like he was about to jump out of it. Hall noticed his actions and made sure to put him back in his place. He balled his hand into a fist and raised it up, ready to unleash it again.

"Go ahead," Hall said. "Just try something. I dare you."

Shafer clenched his jaw tight and glared up at Hall with menacing eyes, clearly not happy with his current situation. But he also knew that he wasn't a match for Hall with the fisticuffs. A minute later, Charlotte returned with someone that worked on the train.

"This young lady said there was some kind of problem here?"

"Yes," Hall replied. "This man here is a wanted criminal named Dustin Shafer. I'd suggest confining him to his room and alerting the authorities that he's here so they can take him into custody."

"I'll alert the police department right away so they can take him when we get to Los Angeles."

Hall looked to Shafer and grinned. "See ya around."

Once they exited the room, the train official locked the room so Shafer couldn't get out before the police came aboard to arrest him. Hall and Charlotte went back to the regular cars and sat down.

"Thanks for being on time this time," Charlotte said.

"Well hey, I didn't wanna leave you alone with him for too long. Never know what might happen."

Charlotte shot him an unpleasant look. "Oh really? You really wanna go there?"

Hall laughed. "Never know."

"Not unless my body is dead and cold."

"That doesn't sound as nice."

"Yeah. Anyway, what's the next move? Train back to Anaheim?"

"No, I think I'm finished with trains for a while. I don't wanna even see a toy train for Christmas."

"So what do we do when we get back there?"

"We finish it."

18

Hall and Charlotte took an hour bus ride back to the Anaheim area, where they then decided on how to successfully enact the final leg of their plan. Hall wanted to meet with Palumbo somewhere, but he wanted it to be a neutral site. Charlotte had found addresses for some of Palumbo's business interests, but Hall wasn't going to just walk into one of those places, assuming that the deck would be stacked against him.

"How are you going to contact him then?" Charlotte asked. Hall just looked at her, giving her one of those famous glances that he gave when he wanted her to do something unpleasant. "Oh no, no, not this time. Now I'm putting my foot down. Those other two guys were one thing, this is something completely different. Palumbo's probably got ten men around him. I'm not doing it."

Hall smiled. "Relax, I was only kidding. I don't want you to do anything."

Charlotte smacked his arm. "You rat. You were purposefully toying with me to get me worked up."

"Yeah, it was kind of funny."

"Glad you think so. But seriously, what's the plan?"

"I think I'll call Kowalski at the club," Hall answered.

"Kowalski? What for?"

"He must know his phone number. Then if he gives it to me, then I'll call Palumbo and tell him I have his bag."

"And do what with it?"

"Some type of trade."

"Oh, good, nothing can go wrong there," Charlotte said, rolling her eyes.

Hall called Kowalski's club, asking for him. He was told the owner was there and to wait a minute. About a minute went by before Kowalski picked up the phone.

"Rex here."

"Hey, it's Hall."

"What do you want?" Kowalski asked, in a gruff sounding voice, though not exactly unfriendly.

"I need Palumbo's number."

"What for?"

"I wanna call him."

"Why?"

"What difference does it make to you?" Hall asked. "You buddies again?"

"Of course not. Just wondering why you'd want to talk to him?"

"I have a proposition for him."

"I can tell you this, he's not interested in any proposition you might give to him. Unless he's getting money out of it."

"Well..."

"What could you possibly have to offer him?"

"I just want to talk to him."

There was silence on both ends of the phone for a few seconds. Kowalski was thinking of why Hall would want to talk to his former partner, and he could only think of one reason. "Wait a minute. Do you have the bag?"

"What makes you say that?"

"Because that's the only reason I can think of that you'd want to talk to him. You're obviously not gonna bargain with him with stuff you ain't got. That's the only thing it could be."

"And what if I do?" Hall said.

"Have you had that the whole time? Were you putting me on?"

"Everything I said to you was completely straight. Palumbo put two decoys on that train, one of which was me. The other was a man named Jayson Wendel."

"Wendel? I know him. He's a Palumbo stooge."

"Yeah, well, I've already dealt with him. Palumbo's plan was to have you chasing me or him for a while, all while the real person holding the bag got away safely."

"And you know who that is?"

"Man named Dustin Shafer."

"Shafer? He's a big time broker."

"Was. I caught up to him a couple hours ago," Hall replied. "He was on his way to Sacramento. I don't really know what the plan was from there, but Mr. Shafer is now in the hands of the Los Angeles Police Department. But not before I took the liberty of relieving Shafer of his bag."

"Did you look inside?"

"I did. I can only assume it's what everyone wants."

"So what are your plans? Hand the bag over to Palumbo in exchange for what? Letting you off the hook?"

"I guess something like that."

Kowalski laughed. "I gotta hand it to you, kid. You certainly got some funny ideas in your head. You're quick with your hands and feet, but your brain, not so fast."

"What's that supposed to mean?"

"If you think you're just gonna hand a bag over to Palumbo and think he's gonna let you walk out of there with your life, you're crazier than I thought you were. You're a liability to him now. You know too much and he's still gonna have to broker a new deal. Whatever you dream up, Palumbo's gonna bring enough muscle to get the job done. And I guarantee he and his boys won't just stand there and let you stomp all over them either. You'll be bringing fists of fury and he'll be bringing lead... and lots of it."

"I can deal with it."

"With who? You and Miss Frying Pan? You'll never make it."

"I want this to end," Hall said. "I didn't ask for this and I don't wanna be caught up in it anymore."

"Well you are caught up in it and the only way out of it is to get rid of that bag."

"That's what I want to do."

"No, you wanna get yourself killed. And that's what you'll do, along with blondie, if you don't rethink your plan."

"You got a better idea?"

"Yeah. You call Palumbo and tell him you wanna deal. I'll tell you the spot to pick. Then when he shows up, me and my boys will be there to meet him."

"You're gonna kill him and take the bag?"

"Well that's what he's planning on doing to you, isn't it? Unless you want that bag all to yourself. Maybe going into business for yourself now?"

"I don't give a damn about this bag," Hall replied. "I don't want it or any money that comes from it."

"Then let's do this together. He screwed both of us over. And we can both get what we want. I'll get that bag and I'll get a hundred percent of it. And you can get your life back. After it's over we both go our separate ways."

"And what makes me think I can trust you? Why

should I believe after it's over that you won't just kill me too?"

"Listen, kid, I've never killed anybody that didn't deserve it or done me wrong. We both want Palumbo, and it'll be tough getting him on my own. He'll have his security around expecting me to do something. But if he's meeting you, he won't expect me. And that's how we can both win."

"That doesn't exactly instill great confidence in me."

"How about we do something like this? You have your girlfriend in a spot outside somewhere? Doesn't matter to me where. Keep her out of sight, but somewhere she can watch the front door. If you don't walk through it after it's over, she calls the police and I get arrested. If you do walk out the door, she puts the phone away and we all go our separate ways."

Hall thought about his offer for a minute. He really didn't like being involved in the killing of anybody, even setting them up for it, but he also knew it was probably the only way he was ever going to get free of this. It had to be done. He was in too deep now, knew too much.

"All right, deal."

Kowalski then gave Hall the phone number for Palumbo. Kowalski also told him the place he wanted to do this thing at, giving him the address of an abandoned warehouse that he'd used many times before. Kowalski knew it well and knew there were places they could get a good position behind. Wanting the exchange to go down in three hours, it'd also give Kowalski some time to prepare and get his boys together.

Listening to the conversation, and judging by the tone of Hall's words, Charlotte could tell something was up. And she wasn't sure she liked it. "What's going on?"

"I got Palumbo's number."

"And what'd you have to give up to get it?"

"What makes you think I gave up anything?"

"Because Rex Kowalski doesn't seem like the kind of man who gives up anything of value for free."

Hall looked at her, knowing she wouldn't like what he was about to tell her. "We'll set up a meet with Palumbo at a place that Kowalski knows."

"Why?"

"He wants to be there."

"Why?" Charlotte sternly asked, knowing there was more and that Hall was holding back.

Hall licked his lips before he began answering. "Because we're not going to make any kind of deal with Palumbo. We're a loose end as far as he's concerned. He's not just gonna let us walk from this. We know too much."

"OK? So how does Kowalski come in?"

"Him and Palumbo are at odds, he wants the bag, we've got it, he's willing to give us protection in order to get it."

"So basically he's gonna throw down with Palumbo in order to get the bag?"

"Yeah."

"And we can trust him...? How?"

"All he wants is that bag," Hall replied.

"We'll still know everything about him though."

"I think he's on the level. He gets the bag, we get our lives back, everyone goes their separate ways and no one ever has to talk about this again."

Charlotte raised one of her eyebrows, clearly not having the same level of trust that Hall did. She felt that was a big leap of faith to put that much belief in a criminal who'd chased them not too long ago. Hall then called Palumbo, the last piece of the puzzle that he needed to fit in. A man answered after the third ring.

"Hello?"

"Palumbo?"

"Who do I have the pleasure of speaking with?"

"This is Brandon Hall. You already know who I am."

"Indeed I do. How did you get my number?"

"That's irrelevant right now," Hall said, not wanting to waste time aimlessly chatting away. He wanted to get right to the point and dictate terms so that Palumbo didn't have a choice but to comply with them. He also didn't want to engage in dialogue and have Palumbo try to smooth talk his way into something different than what Hall wanted. "What is relevant is that I have what you want."

"And what is that?"

"A certain black bag that you had traveling on a train with Dustin Shafer."

There was silence on Palumbo's end of the phone, obvious concern for what had happened.

"That's right. I've got it."

"And Mr. Shafer?" Palumbo asked.

"He's currently dealing with the Los Angeles Police Department."

"And how did that happen?"

"That's inconsequential to what we need to talk about. I have the bag, you want it, and if you want it back, you'll meet me at the time and place that I say."

"And what are your terms?"

"You give me your word, plus fifty thousand dollars, that you'll never bother me again, and I'll surrender the bag to you."

Hall could hear a slight laugh by Palumbo on the other end of the phone. He knew Palumbo probably thought the terms were extremely small and ridiculous, but it didn't really matter. Hall just needed him to show up. He didn't wait for Palumbo to answer though, before giving him the time and place of the meeting.

"You've only got one chance at this," Hall said. "If you're even five minutes late, I'm gone, and this bag's going to the authorities."

"I will be there."

Hall hung up, thinking that went about as well as he could have hoped for. Though he seemed to have a pleased look on his face, Charlotte did not share the same attitude.

"So when's all this happening?" Charlotte asked, knowing it was pointless to argue or debate.

"Three hours. And we need to get a backpack."

"Why?"

"Just in case we can't actually trust any of them, I'm not actually walking in there with the stuff. I'll carry in an empty bag and put the real stuff in the backpack."

"Smart. Where's the backpack gonna be?"

"Out with you."

"Out with me?" Charlotte said, not liking being split apart. "Why can't I be with you?"

"It's gonna be too dangerous for both of us to be in there and there's likely going to be a lot of shooting."

"So what about you?"

"It's not gonna work without me being there."

Upset about the prospect of losing him, she reached over and put her arms around him, burying her head in his chest. Hall put his arms around her and put his hand on the back of his head, lowering his face until it touched her hair.

"If anything happens to me, you just take that bag to the police and tell them everything."

Charlotte pulled her head off his chest, though they still had their arms around each other. "Why can't we just do that now?"

"Because there's no guarantee that Palumbo won't come after me again or use me again. I don't really wanna worry or look over my shoulder for the rest of my life wondering if he's coming again."

A couple tears started coming out of Charlotte's eyes, though she did her best to control them.

"Hey, you're not gonna get rid of me just yet," Hall said, wiping the tears off her cheeks. Charlotte just buried her head back into his chest as they stood there holding each other. Hall wished this embrace was under very different circumstances. He would have enjoyed it more if there wasn't the looming threat of death around the corner. "Everything's going to be OK."

19

Just before getting to the warehouse, Hall called Kowalski again, just to make sure he wasn't there yet. It was about an hour before the scheduled meeting time, and Hall wanted to survey the area first to make sure there was a good spot for Charlotte to hide. The building was in the middle of an industrial complex and there were other buildings nearby, including one across the street. They parked the car around the back of that building, out of sight, as they looked for a spot to enter. They eventually found a broken window, Hall smashing the rest of it so they could climb through it.

Since it was also empty, and it was later at night, they didn't have to worry about someone sneaking up on Charlotte without Hall being there. They wandered around the building for a few minutes, trying to find the best spot for her. They eventually found some steps and went up to the third floor, finding a window that gave Charlotte a perfect vantage point.

"Remember, if you see Palumbo or Kowalski walk out of that building without me, then assume I didn't make it," Hall said. Charlotte closed her eyes at the thought of it. "If that happens, you immediately call the police to get them here on the double. Otherwise, those guys are gonna start looking for you."

Charlotte sighed and nodded, more concerned about him at the moment. She didn't even want to think about the possibility of him not making it.

"Are you sure there's not another way?"

"Everything's gonna work out," Hall said. "I promise."

Charlotte was hoping that he'd give her a kiss on the lips to make her feel better, but it wasn't coming. Not that Hall wouldn't have liked to, but not under these circumstances. If he did it now, it would have almost seemed like he was saying goodbye, in case he didn't make it. And he wasn't going to think in those terms, even if he knew it was a real possibility. He didn't want her to think like that either.

"I'll be back."

Hall then went back downstairs and exited the building, hustling to the car to get the now empty black bag. He rushed around to the front and crossed a road to get to the warehouse. Once he got there, he found one of the front doors locked. Charlotte was watching him from her window, observing him going to the side of the building and out of sight. She hoped that it wouldn't be the last time she saw him. Hall found a side door unlocked and went inside.

It was a pretty dimly lit building, which he expected since it was no longer in use except for Kowalski's illegal dealings. Hall walked around to get an idea of the floor plan so he could have a plan of where to go if things got heavy and out of hand quickly. The first floor was opened up towards the middle with not much in the way, a few loose boxes here and there, but nothing that could be used for a shield if need be. There were a few large crates lined against the walls in every direction. Hall couldn't help but think they were lined up in a way that seemed to perfect. He wouldn't have been surprised if Kowalski had strategically placed them that way so he could have a jump on his opponents.

Hall looked up at the second floor and it was still open towards the middle, though there was a balcony and railing that went all the way around the entire floor, so someone could be stationed up there and look down at the proceedings happening below them. Though Hall was mostly trying to get a feel for the place, he was also making sure nobody else was there. He'd hated to have gotten shot in the back for being careless as to not check the place out. After checking every room, though, he was indeed alone. But not for long.

Kowalski and his crew of four others, including

Ricky, Benny, and the two that waited for Hall in his apartment showed up. Hall was standing in the middle of the warehouse when one of the front doors opened, a sliver of line shining in through the opening. Kowalski and his boys walked over to Hall and met him in the middle of the floor.

"How'd you get in?"

"Side door," Hall answered. "It was already open."

"Benny, check the place out."

"I've already done that. There's no one else here."

"All right, good." Kowalski looked at the time and saw they had about forty-five minutes until Palumbo was supposed to show. "You boys start taking up your positions." He then observed the black bag on the floor next to Hall's foot. "I take it that's the merchandise?"

Hall nodded. "Yep."

"Mind if I take a look at it?"

"When this is over."

"Fair enough."

Ricky and another man took up positions behind crates on the first floor, each going to an opposite side. Benny took the other man and went up to the second floor and spread out so they could get a good view. Kowalski stayed next to Hall for a few minutes.

"We got about forty minutes," Kowalski said. "Palumbo usually arrives for all meetings about five minutes early. Sometimes ten if he decides to scout around first if he doesn't trust who he's meeting."

"Let's just assume thirty-five then. How many men's he gonna bring with him?"

"Tough to say. Could be as little as three. Might be as much as ten. Really all depends on his mood and how much firepower he thinks he needs. I'm thinking it'll be somewhere around five or six."

"He ever been here before?"

"Once, about a year ago. Those were under happier times."

"Where are you gonna be?"

"Behind that crate on the far wall."

"Just try to remember what you're shooting at," Hall said. "I'd hate to get shot as a case of mistaken identity."

Kowalski grinned. "Just remember to duck."

Kowalski then left to take up his position. It was a long wait for everyone involved, but nobody more than Charlotte, if only for the reason that she was out of the loop on everything. She had no idea what was going on inside that warehouse or what they were planning. The next half hour that passed felt like a lifetime for her, not having communication from anybody.

About ten minutes before the meeting time, Charlotte saw two black SUV's zoom by and pull in just in front of the warehouse. Four large men got out of the first one, but she didn't recognize Palumbo. The men just milled around for a minute, looking at their surroundings, seemingly looking for signs of trouble. With the coast clear, one of the men went over to the second SUV and opened one of the back doors. Palumbo then stepped out, Charlotte clearly recognizing his face. Three other men also stepped out. They all huddled around their leader for a minute, getting last-minute instructions.

Charlotte got her phone ready, figuring the least she could do was give Hall a heads up on how many there were, even though they hadn't discussed her doing that beforehand. Three of Palumbo's men split up from the main group, going around the side of the building. Charlotte sent Hall a quick text to let him know, hoping he hadn't turned his phone off. Luckily, Hall kept his phone on and got the message. He immediately let the others know.

"Listen up," Hall shouted. "Palumbo's here with seven men. Three are going around the side or the back."

"Benny, hear that?" Kowalski asked.

"Yeah," Benny replied.

"You take the three on the side. We'll take the ones up front."

"Got it."

Only a minute later, Palumbo entered the warehouse, though he wound up coming in last. If bullets started flying, he certainly wasn't going to get one first. Palumbo's men stayed put as he moved past him, seeing Hall in the middle of the room. Palumbo was still on his guard at first.

"Where is your friend? The pretty blonde one."

"She's around," Hall replied.

"Have her come out so I can see her."

"No. Maybe she's in a spot to take you out in case you try something."

Palumbo laughed, finding it hysterical. "What is she, some kind of sniper or something?"

"Make a wrong move and find out."

Palumbo laughed some more. "You have confidence and guts. I like that combination. Perhaps you would like to work for me. I could use a man like you."

"No thanks."

"I'll pay you good money."

"I prefer to earn mine legally."

"Suit yourself," Palumbo pleasantly said. He started walking in Hall's direction. "I see you have my bag with you."

"Bring my money?"

"Well there was a slight complication with that. Turns out the bank was not open. I will get it for you tomorrow."

"That's not the deal."

"I have decided to alter the deal."

As soon as the words left his lips, Palumbo's three men came in through the side entrance, making themselves visible. Hall heard the door shut and turned around, noticing them immediately.

"You see, I choose not to do business and pay people who take what is rightfully mine," Palumbo said. "So I will just take the bag."

"If you want it, you gotta come and get it."

Palumbo looked at one of his men and nodded for him to get the bag. The man immediately went over to Hall and grabbed the bag. Hall gave him no resistance in taking it. As the man turned around to come back to his leader, he thought the bag felt light and stopped, taking a look inside.

"It's empty!"

Hall immediately hurled himself at the man, knocking him over. As the two wrestled on the ground, Kowalski and his men opened fire. Though a couple of Palumbo's men instantly perished, the rest of them withdrew their weapons and took cover to fire back. As they exchanged a barrage of gunfire, Hall had gotten the better of his opponent. He was trying to keep as low as possible, worried about taking a stray bullet, considering he was in the middle of the room and in the line of fire.

Once his opponent was no longer a threat, Hall crawled quickly to get to what he hoped was a safer spot. When he got there, he instantly heard the screams of men who'd met an early demise. One of Kowalski's men fell over the railing after getting shot. Another one had fallen to the floor behind one of the crates that did not protect him as well as he thought it would. Several of Palumbo's men had also been killed.

Hall peeked his head around some boxes to see what was going on as it seemed like the gunfire was never-ending. Not even two seconds would go by without the sound of gunfire ripping through the air. Hall looked up when he heard a loud screeching sound as Benny had been shot and killed, himself also falling over the railing. A loud thud was heard as his body hit the ground.

"Benny!" Ricky yelled, his body moving away from the cover of the crate just a few inches to get a better look at his friend, hoping that he was miraculously still alive somehow. It was a fatal mistake though, as it gave Palumbo's men enough of a target to shoot at, and Ricky also took several lethal shots to the chest, instantly falling over onto some cardboard boxes for his final resting spot.

Kowalski, seeing his friends all dead now, became enraged. He sprung up from his spot, surprising the two men left along the side door, killing them before they knew what hit them. There were still two men left, and Hall knew Kowalski would need some help. With Palumbo, and the two other men focused on the armed Kowalski, Hall slid along the side wall to get to their position. They didn't notice him coming, and once he was within range, Hall jumped on top of Palumbo, pulling him down to the ground.

Both of Palumbo's men looked down, waiting for a clear shot to save their boss. Taking their eyes off Kowalski was their last mistake though, as he was almost on top of them by the time they looked back up at him. After delivering headshots on the both of them, Kowalski focused his attention on the two men on the ground. After only a few seconds, Hall stood up, pulling Palumbo up with him as he grabbed his shirt. Hall was about to deliver a few more blows, but instantly halted his attack as two more shots rang out. He flinched as he looked up at Kowalski.

"Sorry," Kowalski said. "Don't have time to drag things out."

Hall then looked back down at Palumbo, blood pouring out of the two new holes that were just put into his chest. Hall then turned his head, observing blood and death everywhere he looked.

"Very costly," Kowalski said, walking over to Benny's lifeless body.

"Was it worth it?" Hall asked.

Kowalski turned back to him. He just shrugged, not really having an answer. "It's just the way it goes. We all know the risks when we get into this business. And we know this result is a possibility for all of us. Just the way it is."

"I guess so."

Kowalski then walked over to the black bag and picked it up, looking inside. He then tossed it aside. "We had a deal."

Hall nodded. "We still do."

"Then where is it?"

"It's outside."

Hall and Kowalski then exited the warehouse and stood just outside the front doors for a minute.

"So where is it?" Kowalski asked, a little impatient.

"Relax. Should be coming in a minute."

"Oh, I get it. Insurance policy. Your little blonde-haired friend is waiting out here somewhere with the stuff. Once she sees that you're safe and sound, she brings it up. Smart."

"I trust that you'll uphold your end of the bargain."

"Trust me, kid, you'll never see me again." Kowalski even let out the slightest hint of a smile. "Once I get the money, I might even buy some mansion in some foreign country, leave all this behind and live like a king for the rest of my life."

"Sounds like a good plan."

They heard the sound of a car coming closer and started to breathe a sigh of relief. The ordeal for all of them was almost over. As soon as Charlotte pulled up and stopped the car, she jumped out of the car and ran over to Hall to give him a hug.

Hall smiled at her. "I told you everything would be OK."

Kowalski interrupted their moment, wanting to get on with things. "Hey, let's move this along. You two can get a hotel room later if you want."

Charlotte, not able to wipe the smile off her face, continued looking at Hall. "Should I get it?"

"Yeah."

Charlotte ran back to the car and opened the back door, reaching onto the seat to grab the backpack. Just as she closed the door, a horrified look came over her face as she saw an armed man in the frame of the door.

"Brandon!"

Hall and Kowalski both turned back toward the warehouse to see the pending threat. Just as they turned, the armed man opened fire, hitting Kowalski several times. As he fell to the ground, Hall ran back to the car and Charlotte, wanting to shield her from any harm. Before he got there, Kowalski rolled over on the ground, returning fire against the man in the door. The two simultaneously fired several shots. The man in the door slumped to the ground, holding his stomach as his hands were soon covered in blood. He perished only seconds later.

Hall and Charlotte stood by the car, almost in shock at what just happened. They weren't sure what to do next. They certainly had no loyalty or warm feelings toward anyone there. Most people probably would have just left.

"C'mon, let's just go," Charlotte said.

"No, not yet," Hall replied.

Hall walked over to Kowalski's body, which was now riddled with bullets. Hall got up to five, then stopped counting. The man was in bad shape and probably wasn't going to make it much longer. Hall knelt down by his side. Kowalski looked up at him and tried to laugh, though he only wound up coughing up blood. He then gave Hall a smile, seeming OK with his fate.

"Looks like I'm not gonna get that mansion after all."

As Kowalski's eyes closed, and he stopped breathing, Hall looked over at Charlotte and just shook his head to let her know he was gone. Hall stood up and took one last look at the warehouse. All that pain and death over money. He shook his head, not understanding why some men would throw everything away, including their life.

Hall and Charlotte got back in their car and headed back to their apartments. They figured they'd take a little time to unwind from everything, clean up their apartments, then turn the backpack over to the police. Once they got back to the complex, they went to Charlotte's apartment first. As they walked in, it felt like forever since they'd been there last.

"Seems like so long ago," Charlotte said.

As Hall closed the door behind him, he stopped in the middle of the room and stared at Charlotte, not taking his eyes off her. She turned around and caught him staring.

"Why are you looking at me like that?"

"I was just thinking, years from now, when people ask us how we first met, we'll really have a heck of a story to tell them."

Charlotte moved a little closer to him. "Oh we will, huh? What makes you think we'll be together at all in a few years?"

Hall started blushing, thinking maybe he spoke out of turn. Charlotte then gave him that flirty smile of hers. The two of them moved closer to each other and put their arms around each other's waists as they gazed into each other's eyes.

"You know, there's something that I've really been wanting to do," Hall said.

"Oh yeah? What's that?" Charlotte replied, their faces coming closer together.

"I really just wanna.... we haven't known each other long and... would you mind if I kissed you?"

Charlotte let out a laugh as their lips finally touched each other. "After all we've been through, I'd be pretty pissed off if you didn't."

ABOUT THE AUTHOR

Mike Ryan lives in Pennsylvania with his wife, and four kids. He's the bestselling author of The Silencer Series, as well as numerous other books. Visit his website at www.mikeryanbooks.com to find out more about his books, as well as sign up for his newsletter.

ALSO BY MIKE RYAN

Continue with Book 2 of the Brandon Hall Series:

Hard Bargain

Also By Mike Ryan:

The Silencer Series

The Extractor Series

The Eliminator Series

The Cain Series

The Ghost Series

A Dangerous Man

The Last Job

The Crew

Printed in Great Britain
by Amazon